The Sleepover Club

Three fantastic Sleepover Club
stories in one!

Have you been invited to all these sleepovers?

Mega

Sleepover Club ②

The Sleepover Club at Rosie's
The Sleepover Club at Kenny's
Starring the Sleepover Club

Rose Impey
Narinder Dhami

HarperCollins *Children's Books*

The Sleepover Club at Rosie's first published in Great Britain by Collins 1997
The Sleepover Club at Kenny's first published in Great Britain by Collins 1997
Starring the Sleepover Club first published in Great Britain by Collins 1997

First published in this three-in-one edition by HarperCollins *Children's Books* 2000

HarperCollins *Children's Books* is a division of HarperCollins*Publishers* Ltd
77-85 Fulham Palace Road, Hammersmith
London W6 8JB

The HarperCollins *Children's Books* website address is www.harpercollinschildrensbooks.co.uk

6

The Sleepover Club at Rosie's
The Sleepover Club at Kenny's
Text copyright © Rose Impey 1997

Starring the Sleepover Club
Text copyright © Narinder Dhami 1997

Original series characters, plotlines and settings © Rose Impey 1997

ISBN-13   978 0 00 710903 6
ISBN-10   0 00 710903-2

The authors assert the moral right to be identified as the authors of the work.
Printed and bound in Great Britain by Clays Ltd, St Ives plc

Sleepover Kit List

1. Sleeping bag
2. Pillow
3. Pyjamas or a nightdress
4. Slippers
5. Toothbrush, toothpaste, soap etc
6. Towel
7. Teddy
8. A creepy story
9. Food for a midnight feast:
   chocolate, crisps, sweets, biscuits.
   In fact anything you like to eat.
10. Torch
11. Hairbrush
12. Hair things like a bobble or hairband,
    if you need them
13. Clean knickers and socks
14. Change of clothes for the next day
15. Sleepover diary and membership card

The Sleepover Club at Rosie's

THE PET SHOW

CHAPTER ONE

Oh, hi there. You haven't seen my dog, Pepsi, have you? She's gone missing. She's a black spaniel. She's escaped lots of times before and someone always brings her back. The trouble is that this time she's in season and, if we don't find her soon, you know what *that* could mean. My mum's in a real razz with me! I didn't mean to leave the front gate open.

The thing is, last week I had this big argument with her and Dad because they won't let Pepsi have puppies. It's bad enough they won't let *me* have a brother or sister, now they won't let the dog have a baby either!

So Mum thinks I let Pepsi out on purpose. Dad'll go ballistic when he knows. It would have to happen just now, when I was in their good books for a change.

I know, why don't you come with me to look for Pepsi, then I can tell you about our latest Sleepover Club adventure? That was all to do with pets. It was excellent. Come on, we'll head for the park, that's one of Pepsi's favourite places, and I'll tell you all about it on the way.

It all started with the Pet Show in the Village Hall. It was organised to raise money for an animal refuge and the whole Sleepover Club decided to enter. We first heard about it at Brownies a few weeks ago. We all go to Brownies, everyone in the Sleepover Club, even Fliss and Lyndz who are old enough to go up to Guides if they want to, but they're waiting for the rest of us. We like to stick together. Can you remember who everyone is?

First there's Laura Mackenzie – we call her Kenny. She's my best friend.

Felicity Sidebotham – we call her Fliss. Oh boy, I'm glad I'm not called Sidebotham. She gets teased all the time.

Then there's Lyndsey Collins – we call her Lyndz. It was Lyndz that got us into trouble this time, or at least her dog, Buster, did. He's a menace.

And Rosie Cartwright. The sleepover was at Rosie's, which was totally cool because she's never let us stay at her place before and her house is perfect for sleepovers: big and old and a bit spooky.

That just leaves me – Francesca Theresa Thomas, but you can call me Frankie.

So, that's all of us. Yeah, yeah, I know five's not a good number, someone's bound to get left out, but five's how many there are, so that's that.

Now, back to the story. Brown Owl showed us some posters about the Pet Show and asked us each to take one home and put it up somewhere. She said she wanted all of us who have pets to go in for it as part of our Pet Lovers Badge. I couldn't wait to ask Mum and Dad if I could take Pepsi. I was sure I'd win, but then so were all the others. And the trouble was three of us have dogs. We started arguing straight away, as soon as Brown Owl had finished.

"Buster's so smart he's bound to win," said Lyndz. She's got this weird little Jack Russell terrier, he's absolutely mad. You should see him.

"Dream on," I said. "He's not that smart and he won't beat Pepsi. She's so cute."

"Well," said Rosie, "Jenny's smart *and* she's cute."

Which is true. Jenny's a mongrel, but she's got a lot of sheepdog in her. Her coat's really shiny, black and white and she's got a wonderful big tail. And she's clever, too. So that made me mad. But Fliss made me even madder.

"Well, you can't all win," she said, smiling.

"Oh, very good," I said. "Now tell us something we don't know."

"I might win," said Kenny.

Kenny doesn't have a dog, although she'd love one, but she's had loads of other pets. She had a hamster once, and a rabbit, but they both died. And a cat called Tinkerbell, which ran away, and a bird called Bobby which flew out of the window, and a goldfish, which the cat ate before she ran away. She's not had much luck so far.

Now she's got a big white rat called Merlin. She says he's mega-intelligent and she's training him, but he doesn't seem to have learnt much! There's something about the way Kenny lets him sit on her shoulder that gives me the heebie-jeebies.

Kenny's sister, Molly the Monster, shares a bedroom with Kenny and she hates rats, so Merlin has to live in the garage. I know Kenny's my best friend and everything but, to be honest, I agree with Molly; I wouldn't want to sleep in a room with a rat either.

The Pet Show wasn't only for dogs, of course, you could take other pets. On the poster it said there were prizes in each different class: hamsters, rabbits, cats, and lots of others, but there was no mention of rats!

"It's not fair," said Kenny. "What about Merlin?"

"Don't worry, Laura," said Brown Owl. "I'll find out if rats are allowed."

So that just left Fliss, who was a real problem, because Fliss doesn't have a pet at all, apart from her goldfish, Bubbles. And you can't do much with a goldfish, can you?

The Pet Show

"It's just not fair," she said. "My mum's so mean."

Fliss's mum is not mean, she's just mega house-proud.

"You have loads of things we don't have," I reminded her. "You've got more clothes than Princess Di for a start."

"And toys..." said Lyndz.

"And CDs..." said Kenny.

"OK, OK, but I haven't got a pet to take to the Pet Show and you lot have."

Which was true and we couldn't seem to think of a way round it. Anyway, there was no point in us arguing about which one of us was going to win because we already knew who would. You didn't have to be a genius to work that out.

CHAPTER TWO

"The dreaded M&Ms," said Kenny. We all made being-sick noises.

It was lunchtime and we were sitting on the steps in the studio at school with just the spotlights on. We were supposed to be working on a dance routine for assembly but we were having a rest.

"Why would they win?" said Rosie. She's new to our school, so she doesn't know all about the M&Ms yet.

"Because they win everything," said Fliss.

Have I told you about the M&Ms?

They're in our class at school and, as if that isn't bad enough, they go to Brownies as well. Their real names are Emma Hughes and Emily Berryman, but we call them the M&Ms. Or sometimes The Queen and The Goblin. I'll tell you why:

Emma Hughes is tall and soppy and really annoying, but she's everybody's favourite: our teacher's, the headteacher's, the dinner ladies', Brown Owl's, Snowy Owl's... *And* all the boys like her. She always gets the best marks and gold stars and wins competitions like the Brownie Cook's Challenge and gets picked to be milk monitor and take the register. She is so stuck up. That's why we call her The Queen.

Emily Berryman's nearly as bad. She's dead small, with big eyes and a deep, gruff voice, so we call her The Goblin. She always gets good marks and wins things too. We don't know how they do it. We think it's because they cheat, but we haven't been able to prove it. Not yet, anyway.

The worst thing about them is the way they whisper and giggle. They are seriously gruesome. The moment Brown Owl told us about the Pet Show they started giggling and behaving as if they'd already won.

And the annoying thing is they probably will win. Emma Hughes has this dog that she's always bragging about and Emily Berryman has a cat. We've never seen them, but we've heard plenty about them.

The M&Ms are our worst enemies and the thing we hate most in the whole world, the whole universe in fact, is being beaten by them.

"We've got to think of a way to stop them," I said.

"How?" said Lyndz. "I don't think Pepsi and Buster stand much of a chance against Duchess of Drumshaw The Third and Sabrina Sprightly Dancing."

Can you believe those names? I didn't make them up. I don't suppose that's what they call them everyday, when they take them out for walks or call them for their food. That would be too stupid, even for them. But those are their pedigree names and when they're showing off that's what they call them.

"Pepsi's a pedigree spaniel," I said, "but she doesn't have a stupid name like that." She's the best dog in the world and I love her to bits. She's got a black curly coat and long ears that trail on the ground and the saddest eyes in the world. Sometimes she looks at me as if I've just eaten the last Rolo.

I tell Pepsi everything and she tells me all her secrets. That's how I know she wants puppies! But when I tried to tell Mum that, she said, "Francesca, for the last time, I have told you, the answer is NO! Pepsi is getting too old to have puppies."

"Yeah, even her ears are going grey," said Kenny.

"So?" I said.

"Well, grey ears might stop her winning the Pet Show," said Lyndz.

"Hmm," I said. "I can't see High-Jumping Dog winning either." That's what we sometimes call Lyndz's dog, Buster.

He's got these stumpy little legs, but he can jump up and reach a Smacko even when Lyndz holds it high over her head. It's as if he's got spring-loaded feet. And when he walks he looks like a little clockwork toy.

"I suppose he is a bit wild," Lyndz giggled.

"Jenny's our best hope of winning," said Kenny. "Even though she's a mongrel."

Rosie didn't like Kenny calling Jenny a mongrel. "She's mostly sheepdog," she said. "She can do all sorts of tricks and she's brilliant with Adam."

Adam is Rosie's brother, he's in a wheelchair.

For ages Rosie wouldn't let us go to her house and, like idiots, we thought it was because she felt embarrassed about Adam. Then we found out it was nothing to do with Adam, she was embarrassed because her house was such a tip. Actually, it's not really a tip; it just needs decorating. Now she lets us go round all the time.

Adam can't walk and he can't talk because he's got cerebral palsy, I think that's how you spell it. It means his brain was damaged when he was born, but he's such a laugh. He loves jokes and playing tricks on Rosie. For instance, all their doors swing both ways, so that he can push through in his wheelchair. So he goes through in front of her and then lets it go with his feet so it whips back fast and nearly knocks her over.

Jenny, their dog, seems to know exactly what Adam wants even though he can't talk. She brings him things. And she plays football with him.

Adam's mad about football. He can't use his hands because... I don't know why, they sort of jerk about and he can't stop them. But he can kick a football and Jenny runs after it and brings it back. She's so clever.

Some days, after school, Rosie brings Jenny to the park, where I walk Pepsi. They love playing together and it seems really mean to me just having one dog. I'm an only child so I know how that feels! I've tried telling my mum and dad, but they seem to go deaf whenever I get onto that subject.

But at least I've got a dog. Fliss had no pet to take, as she kept on reminding us.

"It's just not fair, I'm sick of hearing about pet shows."

Sometimes Fliss is a real moaner. I call her the Mona Lisa.

"At least we've all got one thing to look forward to," I reminded her. "Tomorrow's our first sleepover at Rosie's."

"Humph," Fliss grunted. "It's the night before the Pet Show, so I know what'll happen: you'll be talking about it all night and leaving me out."

"No, we won't," Rosie promised.

"If you like, we won't even mention the word pets," I said.

"Do you promise?" she said, satisfied at last.

The others nodded and made the Brownie promise, but in fact we needn't have bothered, because the next day Rosie had her brainwave about Gazza, the class hamster. And in the end he came to the sleepover too.

CHAPTER THREE

It was Friday, the day before the Pet Show and the day of the sleepover at Rosie's. Kenny and Lyndz had spent the dinner hour cleaning out Gazza's cage. It was their turn on the rota. If you're thinking that Gazza's a dumb name for a hamster, well, it is. The boys in our class chose it. We wanted Cuddles, but we were outvoted.

Fliss had started up *again* about how unfair everything was. So Rosie said, "Fliss, if your mum won't let you have a pet of your own, why don't you ask her if you can take Gazza home one weekend?"

Fliss looked doubtful but everyone else thought it was a great idea.

"Yeah. Neat," said Kenny. "What about this weekend?"

I jumped down to check the rota to see whose turn it was, in case it was someone who might swap with Fliss. "Uh, oh," I said, shaking my head. "It's Alana Banana."

Mrs Weaver walked in just then and gave me one of her looks. She doesn't like us calling each other names, but that is what we call her: Alana Banana Palmer.

"I was just saying, it's Alana's turn to take Gazza home this weekend," I said.

Alana looked up surprised to hear her name, then she went bright pink. She said she'd forgotten to tell Mrs Weaver she couldn't take him, because they were going away for the weekend. I think Alana's really dippy. Mrs Weaver tutted, you could tell she thought so too.

"OK, now we have a problem."

But before anyone else had time to volunteer Emma Hughes pushed to the front.

"That's alright, Mrs Weaver, I'll take him," she said.

"Are you sure, Emma?"

She nodded and gave her one of those *stoopid* sickly smiles she does which make us really mad.

"Oh, yes. It isn't a problem. Mummy won't mind."

But then, suddenly, without asking Fliss about it, Kenny said, "Fliss would like to take him, Mrs Weaver. She's never had a chance before. Emma's taken him lots of times." Emma Hughes gave Kenny such a look but Kenny ignored her.

"Is that true, Felicity?" Mrs Weaver asked. Fliss went pink, but she nodded.

"Do you need to check with your mum?"

Fliss looked doubtful for a moment but Kenny gave her a dig in the ribs. "Oww! No, I think it'll be OK."

"Good. Well, I'm sure Emma doesn't mind if Felicity has a turn," said the teacher, turning round to find the register. "That seems only fair."

The look on the M&Ms' faces was too good to miss. We stood in a row and smiled back at them as if butter wouldn't melt in our mouths, as my gran says.

"Everyone sit down now," said the teacher. We went back to our table feeling really pleased with ourselves.

"Yeah. One-nil!" said Kenny. "That showed those M&Ms."

But Fliss was already looking worried. "I don't know why you made me say that," she hissed at Kenny. "I'll be in real doom when my mum finds out."

That was when Rosie made her great offer: "Don't worry. You can bring him to my house, if you like. You can play with him there and you won't feel so left out."

"Honest?" said Fliss, she couldn't believe her ears. "Won't your mum mind?"

"No," said Rosie. "It'll be fine."

Fliss started to grin. "You're my best friend ever!" she told Rosie.

"Oh, p-lease," I said. Kenny rolled her eyes, Rosie went bright red.

Then Fliss hugged her, which made her even redder. Rosie's still a bit shy of us. She's quite new to our club. She only moved into Cuddington last summer and into our class when we came back after the summer holidays. At first she seemed a bit of a sad case, but then we found out why.

Rosie's dad had left them a few weeks after they moved in, because he'd met someone else. As if that wasn't bad enough, he'd started to do the house up but then just left them in the middle of it. It looked a bit like a building site, really.

That's why Rosie wouldn't let us

The Pet Show

sleepover at hers, because everywhere was in a mess, especially her bedroom. We kept telling her it didn't matter and in the end she changed her mind. She gave us these neat invitations. Adam did them for her on his computer. I've still got mine. Do you want to see it?

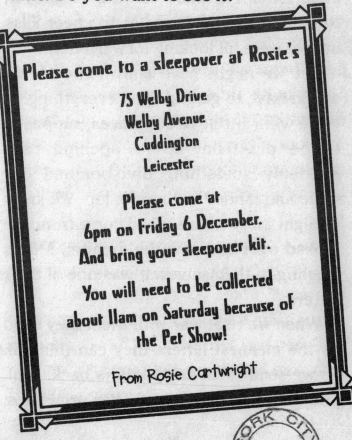

Please come to a sleepover at Rosie's

75 Welby Drive
Welby Avenue
Cuddington
Leicester

Please come at
6pm on Friday 6 December.
And bring your sleepover kit.

You will need to be collected
about 11am on Saturday because of
the Pet Show!

From Rosie Cartwright

I was really looking forward to it because Rosie's house is ever so big with lots of rooms. Some of them are only used for storing stuff, which means loads of places to hide and make dens. It's magic. In fact I couldn't decide which I was more excited about: the Pet Show or the sleepover. Now we'd got the hamster to cheer Fliss up, we were all looking forward to it.

But we might have known the M&Ms would have to go and spoil everything.

We were sitting in our places, supposed to be practising for a spelling test. Suddenly something dive-bombed our table and landed in Kenny's lap. We knew straight away where it had come from. We looked over and saw the dreaded M&Ms giggling to themselves. It was one of their letters.

When we're at war with them they send us the meanest letters they can think of. So we send them nasty letters back. Well, you would, wouldn't you? They print them on the computer so we can't recognise their writing, which is a bit pointless because we know very well it's them and they know very well it's us writing back.

Kenny started to unfold it.

"What does it say?" Fliss squeaked.

"Give me a chance." She smoothed it out and read it aloud to us. "To our enemies. We are watching you. Don't think you'll get away with this. We have put a spell on you. Goodbye forever, Horrible Stinkers."

"What a cheek!" said Lyndz. "We don't stink."

"Right," I said, "after the spelling test we'll ask to go on the computer."

While Mrs Weaver was busy hearing readers, we wrote back to them:

Dear Ugly Mugs,

We hope you both slip down a drain or fall in a bowl of sick. There's no way you will win tomorrow. We'll make sure of that. Have a horrible day, Poshfac

It's funny really, because that is what happened. Not the bit about them falling down the drain or in a bowl of sick, but about them not winning. When we wrote it we didn't have a plan or anything. It was just one of those things you say. And then, when we met them on the way home from school, we said it again. Afterwards we wished we hadn't, because it all turned out to be true.

CHAPTER FOUR

But hang on, before I tell you about that, let's look for Pepsi in the park, there's a few bushes she likes digging around. I can't see her anywhere yet, can you?

Oh, blow. Not a sign. Now where can we try?

I know: the other place she likes is the canal. I'm not allowed to go there on my own, but Dad and I often walk her there. We could go as far as the bridge next to the pub, you can see a long way down on to the towpath from there.

Come on and I'll tell you what happened next.

By the time we'd collected up all Gazza's bits and pieces, we were a bit late leaving school. Rosie put Gazza into his carrying cage and then we helped her carry everything round to her house. We were already loaded down with PE kit, lunchboxes, and school bags. So we must have looked like a travelling circus when we came round the corner of Mostyn Avenue, which is a couple of roads away from Welby Drive, where Rosie lives. Walking towards us were the gruesome M&Ms and who do you think was with them? Only Ryan Scott and Danny McCloud, two horrible boys from our class. That was all we needed.

"Oh, look, it's the Famous Five," said Emma Hughes.

"Which one's the dog?" said Ryan Scott. He thinks he's so funny.

"Ruff, ruff. Here, girls," shouted Danny

McCloud, "fetch a stick." And he broke a whole branch off a tree by the side of the road and threw it at us. Good job for him he missed.

"Oh, very clever," I said. But they'd both started now, whistling and calling us good dogs and silly things like that. Fliss looked like a boiled beetroot with embarrassment. Fliss actually likes Ryan Scott; she says she wants to marry him! She is so weird.

We just kept on walking, pretending we couldn't hear them, but they followed us.

"Dogs are supposed to be kept on a lead," shouted Ryan Scott.

"I've got a good idea," said Emma Hughes, "they could enter each other for the Pet Show. That way they might win."

"Well, you're not gonna win, that's for sure," said Kenny.

"That's what you think," said The Goblin.

"That's what we *know*," said Rosie.

"And how are you going to stop us?" said The Queen.

"Don't you worry, we have our ways," I said, mysteriously.

We all smiled at each other, as if we'd got this big secret that they knew nothing about. We walked off down the road.

"What ways?" Emma Hughes shouted after us.

"You'll find out," Kenny called back to her. Then we carried on down the road trying to ignore the fact that those two stupid dodos were still whistling us to come and the gruesome M&Ms were giggling at them as if they were the funniest things on legs.

Fliss turned to Kenny, "How *are* we going to stop them?"

Kenny shrugged. "Don't ask me," she said, "ask Frankie."

I shrugged too. I had no idea either. But, we'd got them worried and that was almost as good.

* * *

When we reached Rosie's, she was right, her mum didn't mind about Gazza.

"What difference can a hamster make?" she said. "It'll be enough of a madhouse with all you girls round." But she smiled, so we knew she was only kidding.

We were all so excited to be sleeping over at a different house, we raced off home to get our things packed. "See you at seven," Rosie called after us. "Don't be late."

When I got home I gave Pepsi an extra good brush and clean up and told Mum and Dad they'd better keep her like that.

"Don't let her roll in anything on her walk tonight," I warned them.

"Yes, boss," said Dad. "Any more orders while you're away?"

"Yes," I said. "Kindly collect me at eleven in the morning. And don't be late!"

When we arrived at Rosie's we went

straight upstairs and dumped our sleepover kits on her bedroom floor. She's right, her room does look a bit funny with no wallpaper, just plaster on the walls, but her mum lets her put posters up, so it doesn't look boring; it's dead colourful in fact. She's got Oasis, Blur and Leicester City football team, loads of pictures of dogs and people out of the soaps on her walls. Rosie's soppy about soaps.

Her dad's promised to come round soon and decorate, so her mum says she's allowed to write on the walls, which none of the rest of us are allowed to do in our bedrooms.

Rosie said we could help her if we wanted to. It was so cool. We wrote loads of jokes, like *What did the spaceman see in his frying pan? An unidentified frying object. And What do you do if you find a blue banana? Try to cheer it up.*

Rosie said it would certainly cheer her up, when she was lying in bed at night, to read those jokes.

"Just think," I said, "in about a zillion years…"

"When the aliens come," said Lyndz.

"…they might take this wallpaper off and find these jokes."

So then we got into writing messages to Martians and it all got a bit silly. One of them was a bit rude. We had to scribble it out before Rosie's mum saw it. It's a good job we did because just then she came in to tell us to come down for tea.

"Great," said Kenny, "I'm ravishing."

"Don't you mean ravenous?" said Rosie's mum

"I'm ravishing, too," said Kenny, pulling one of her silly faces.

"You're weird, you mean," I said. Then she chased me downstairs to the kitchen. Rosie's mum had laid out a great spread for us with paper cups and plates and fancy serviettes, just like a party. She's dead nice. She's going to college to learn to be a nursery nurse. Rosie has an older sister, Tiffany, but she's always out with her boyfriend, Spud. Her brother Adam was there, though. We're really getting used to Adam now. It was strange at first, talking to someone who can't talk back to you, but Rosie's mum can tell us what he wants to say because he sort of spells it out with his head and she can understand him. So can Rosie some of the time, if he does it slowly.

We had pizza and salad and oven chips, and ice cream for afters. The pizza was OK, but it wasn't a patch on my dad's. The ice cream was heavenly, though: pecan and toffee fudge. Mmm, mmm. Rosie's mum sat and fed Adam, because he can't feed himself, and then she sat him on her knee to give him a drink through one of those baby feeder cups. All the time we were eating he was watching us and listening to what we were saying.

"What are you grinning at?" Rosie said.

Adam stopped drinking because he was choking a bit.

"That's what comes of trying to drink and grin at the same time," said his mum. Then Adam started shaking his head. He was trying to spell something. It was a poem he'd made up, while he'd been watching us have tea. Rosie says he's always making up poems... and jokes. Rosie's mum started spelling it out.

"F-I-V... Five?" she said. Adam nodded then spelt out some more.

"Little... Piggies? Sitting... in... a... row? R-O-S... Rosie's the F-A-T-T..." Rosie started to squeal, "Tell him to stop."

Her mum grinned. "OK, young man, that's enough. Remember your manners."

"You're the little piggy," Rosie told Adam.

"That's about right," their mum said, wiping his chin.

After we'd eaten Rosie said we could

explore her house. There are five bedrooms on the first floor, then a staircase which leads to two more rooms, right up in the roof. In places, I could only just stand up straight without banging my head on the ceiling. The rooms were full of packing cases, cardboard boxes and old bits of furniture. There were no light bulbs up there, so when it started to get dark we couldn't turn on the lights and that made it really spooky.

We played Hide and Seek and Murder in the Dark all over the upstairs and in the attic rooms, squealing and rushing around. There were no light–bulbs up there so we had to use our torches and that made it really spooky. But in no time it was nine o'clock and Rosie's mum came to tell us to get ready for bed. We didn't argue. Actually, we were looking forward to going to bed. That's the best bit.

CHAPTER FIVE

Rosie's room only has one bed in it but it's a double bed. It's coo-ell. None of the rest of us has a doule bed. She's so lucky. We all tried to fit into it, like playing Sardines; we just piled on top of each other. But there was no way we could sleep like that.

"Give me some room," yelled Kenny who was right in the middle. "It's too hot in here."

"I'm falling out," yelled Lyndz.

"Can't you breathe in?" yelled Rosie.

"All night?" I said. "Get real."

So in the end we decided two of us would have to sleep in sleeping bags on the floor. We tossed for it. Oh, g-reat. Guess who lost? Me, of course. And Fliss, who moaned on and on about how it wasn't fair, even though it really was.

After we'd been in the bathroom we sat up in our sleeping bags with our sleepover diaries. At least the rest of us did; Fliss was too busy playing with Gazza.

Kenny was scribbling away like mad, she'd finished before I'd even thought about mine. She slammed her diary shut. "That's me done," she said.

"Read us what you've put," said Lyndz.

"What's it worth?" she said, which is Kenny's favourite question.

"If you do, I'll let you hold Gazza while I write mine," said Fliss.

"Oh, great big hairy deal," said Kenny. But then she said, "OK."

She started to read hers out: "Today is Friday. We are sleeping over at Rosie's house for the first time and it is awesome. I wish I lived here. It's the best." Rosie started to smile; she was dead pleased with that. "Tomorrow, we are going to the Pet Show at the Village Hall and if Merlin wins a rosette I will tie it to his tail. We are at war with the M&Ms... again. They had better look out." She slammed her diary shut and said. "Now, give, give, give, give, give." She held out her hands for the hamster.

"You promised you weren't going to talk about *that*," complained Fliss. But she passed Gazza over while she wrote hers.

Then everyone wanted a turn, so we played Pass the Hamster for a bit. When Rosie went to the bathroom she brought back a toilet roll which was just about used up. She tossed it onto the bed and Kenny put Gazza down so he could wriggle through it, like a tunnel but he seemed more interested in filling his pouches with it.

Next Fliss read us what she'd written: "I haven't got a pet to take to the you-know-what so Rosie is letting me keep Gazza at her house. It is very kind of her. She is my best friend. She can take him out and play with him whenever she likes – as long as she is careful."

Kenny looked at me and rolled her eyes. Sometimes Fliss is unreal. It was then that Rosie came up with her other idea. To tell you the truth, it wasn't such a good idea, but at first we thought it was.

"Why not take Gazza tomorrow?" she said to Fliss. "You can pretend he's yours. No one'll know."

"Yeah, why not?" said Kenny.

I nodded too. I thought it was a great idea, because, if Fliss had a pet to take, it would mean we could talk about the Pet Show, without her moaning on.

"I don't know," said Fliss, doubtfully,

"what if someone recognises him?"

"How would they?" said Rosie. "One hamster looks much like another."

"What if there's anyone from school there?"

We thought about that. It was unlikely our teacher, Mrs Weaver, would be there, but what about other people from our class? And then, as if it had dawned on us all at once, I said, "Oh, no..." and everyone joined in, "The M&Ms."

They'd be sure to recognise Gazza. Those two didn't miss a thing.

"Oh, well, it was a good idea while it lasted," I said.

"Hang on," said Kenny, "You could keep him in a box, or something, until they do the judging. The M&Ms'll be too busy with their own pets. They'll probably be in different rooms. I doubt if they'll put the cats and dogs together with the small pets."

"Yeah. Good thinking, Batman," I said.

You could see Fliss was tempted, but she was still worried about it. Fliss always gets her knickers in a twist if she does anything wrong in case she gets found out. But she really wanted to join in with the rest of us, so in the end she said, "OK, but you've all got to promise not to tell anyone, though."

We all made the Brownie promise and just then Rosie's mum came in and told us to turn off the lights and settle down. I was sure she hadn't heard us but Fliss went bright pink, as if Rosie's mum could read her mind. When she got up to put Gazza in his cage, she dropped him twice. Fortunately both times he landed on the bed. At last she put him in his cage, but she was so nervous she didn't fasten the cage door properly. It was nearly an hour before we realised and by then Gazza had completely disappeared.

After Rosie's mum went out we lay in bed

and counted to twenty-five before we sat up. Sitting up in the dark, with our torches turned on, whispering, is the best thing about sleepovers, I think. Sometimes we tell stories or sing songs or tell jokes. Sometimes we pretend we can talk to ghosts but that can get a bit too scary. Later on, when it's really quiet and we know the grown-ups aren't coming back in, we get out our midnight feast. But it was too early so we decided to finish off our Sleepover Club membership cards.

We'd got some old ones we'd made right at the beginning, but now Rosie's joined we decided we'd make some new ones with photos and everything.

Do you want to see mine? Isn't it excellent? Not as good as Fliss's, though. Hers looks dead posh. She got her mum to take her into Leicester to get a proper passport photo done. The rest of us had to cut up old photographs. I had to cut my face out of a picture at my Uncle Alan's wedding when I was little. Everybody started laughing at it, so I told them what my gran always says, "Small things amuse small minds!"

On the back of the cards we wrote our names, ages, addresses and hobbies. When we'd finished them we signed them. Well, the rest of us did. Kenny did this weird squiggle that looked as if someone had nudged her elbow. Then we passed them round and read each others'.

"I didn't know your hobby was stamp collecting," I said to Fliss.

She went a bit red. "It isn't but I didn't know what else to put. I don't really have a hobby."

The Pet Show

"Course you do," said Lyndz. "You go to Brownies, don't you? You go to dancing classes and gymnastics. You're interested in fashion." She reeled off a few more.

"Oh, I didn't realise *they* were hobbies," said Fliss, grabbing her card back. She's so dozy. She scribbled away and soon ran out of space.

For my hobbies I wrote: Reading, Brownies, Pop Music, Collecting Teddies and Acting. I just *lurv* being in plays. It's the best.

Kenny had written: Football, Swimming, Gymnastics, Snooker, Brownies.

Rosie had put: Netball, (I'd forgotten that), Soaps (she's mad about them), Pop Music and Brownies.

Next I read Lyndz's. She'd written: Horses, Painting, Horses, Brownies, Horses, Cooking Horses.

"Cooking horses?" I said.

"Let me see that." She grabbed it back from me. She'd just missed out the comma. "Oh, very funny, I don't think."

I thought it was very funny, actually, and so did Kenny. We creased up.

Later on, when we were sure Rosie's mum wasn't coming back, we got out the food, put it in a big bowl and passed it round. I'll tell you what there was: sherbet dabs, Black Jacks, Love Hearts, a Snickers bar, six marshmallows and a packet of Original Pringles. We all tucked in straight away.

"D'you think we should give Gazza something?" said Fliss.

"It doesn't seem fair leaving him out," Rosie agreed.

But really there was nothing apart from Pringles we thought a hamster might eat and we weren't really sure about those. We decided we'd try him just with a couple of crumbs to see. Fliss got out of her sleeping bag and went to get him.

That's when we realised he'd gone.

CHAPTER SIX

"He's not here," she wailed. "Oh, help, where is he?"

I jumped up as well, just to check, because Fliss is always losing things, even when they're staring her in the face, but this time she was right: he wasn't there. And when we turned on the lights he wasn't anywhere else we could see either.

We stripped everything off the bed and searched all five sleeping bags. We looked under the bed. We emptied all our sleepover kits out in a pile in the middle of the floor. There were leggings and T-shirts and socks and knickers and slippers and toilet bags and torches and hairbrushes and teddies and sweet packets from the midnight feast. And we still couldn't find him.

Fliss was nearly wetting herself. She kept saying over and over, "I'm going to be in such trouble with Mrs Weaver. I'm going to be in doom forever."

And just then Rosie's mum came back in. "My goodness, what's all this noise?" she said. "Whatever's going on?"

So then we had to tell her, Gazza was gone.

She helped us search the room all over again. But in the end she said, "Well, there's nothing else we can do tonight. We'll just have to hope he comes back when he's hungry. The door's been closed, so he must still be in the room somewhere. We'd just better make sure Jenny doesn't get in here tonight."

"Oh, no," said Fliss horrified. "Would she eat him?"

"Probably not, but the poor hamster might die of fright if he saw her."

"But where can he have gone?" said Fliss, nearly in tears.

"We've looked everywhere, Mum," said Rosie.

"He could be under the floorboards, who knows. Come on, now, let's have this light off and you girls settle down."

"I don't want to sleep on the floor any more," said Fliss.

"I'll swap with you," said Rosie.

So Fliss dragged her sleeping bag onto the bed and Rosie and I got into our sleeping bags on the floor. We cuddled our teddies and Rosie's mum turned out the light.

"It's very late," she said, "I think you should try to go to sleep, now. Goodnight."

For quite a long time, we all lay in the

dark and no one spoke. Rosie kept turning over, Lyndz sucked her thumb, Fliss was sniffing a bit. It sounded as if she was crying. Then I heard Lyndz whisper, "Don't worry. He'll turn up."

"But what if he doesn't?" Fliss sniffed. "I'll be left out again."

I felt sorry for Fliss too but I didn't know what to do. I turned over and tried to get to sleep. I'm always the last to drop off. My brain won't seem to go to sleep for ages after I go to bed, so I was lying there, thinking everyone else was asleep by now, when I heard this noise. It was quite close. In fact it sounded as if it was right underneath my pillow, right under my ear.

Rosie whispered, "Frankie, are you awake?"

"Yes," I whispered.

"Can you hear that noise?"

I could and I knew exactly what it was: Gazza was on the move.

I sat up and turned on my torch. We

crawled out of our sleeping bags and pulled back the carpet. Rosie doesn't have a fitted carpet, like the one in my bedroom. She just has this big square rug in the middle of the floor. We rolled up one side of it and followed the sound and shone our torches down the crack between the floorboards.

"I think I can see him," Rosie hissed. We both got so excited we banged heads. "OW," I yelled. Suddenly all the others were awake.

"What's going on?" said Kenny, jumping out of bed.

"Is it morning?" said Lyndz, rubbing her eyes. She'd only been asleep ten minutes!

"I'm sure I can see him," Rosie said again.

I wasn't sure I could, but I could certainly hear him moving about. Soon the others were crowding round us, Fliss was shivering in her nightie.

"Move back," I said. "You're in the light."

"Try and coax him out with some Pringles," said Kenny, getting one and crumbling it between her fingers. "Look what we've got for you," she said, poking the crumbs down between the floorboards. She posted as much through as she could and waited. But still nothing happened. So we tried some more, until we'd pushed a whole Pringle down.

"If you keep pushing food through to him he'll never come out," said Rosie. "In fact if he eats too much he might get so fat he can't fit back through the hole."

"Good thinking, Wonder Woman," I said. Rosie's pretty clever at times.

Next we tried tapping messages on the floorboards above his head and flashing our torches on and off. But we couldn't get him to come out.

Then Kenny got silly and started shining her torch up Fliss's nightdress.

Fliss shouted, "That's not fair, just because I'm the only one in a nightdress."

So then we shone them up each other's pyjama legs instead, until Rosie hissed at us, "Shhh, my mum'll be in and then there'll be trouble."

I was ready to get back into my sleeping bag anyway, I was getting cold.

"Let's finish off our midnight feast," said Lyndz. But first I made a little trail of food.

Rosie's mum had said Gazza would soon come back if he got hungry. So we crushed up the last few Pringles - there were only three left but as Kenny pointed out that would be a feast for a hamster - and laid them in a trail from the spot where we had heard him, all the way back to his cage.

When all the food was gone Lyndz started dozing off again. Lyndz is always the first to go to sleep. She'd already got her thumb in her mouth and her eyes kept closing. Kenny dug her in the ribs. "Wake up," she said, "let's sing our song before you nod off."

We've got this Sleepover song that we always sing before we go to sleep. I bet you've heard it before.

Down by the river there's a hanky panky

With a bullfrog sitting on the hanky panky

With an Ooh, Aah, Ooh, Aah,

Hey, Mrs Zippy, with a One-two-three...Out!

At the end of each verse one of us lies down. This time I was the one left sitting up in the dark on my own. It felt scary, but in a nice way. You know what I mean?

I turned off my torch and snuggled down into my sleeping bag. I must have fallen asleep straight away and I didn't wake up until the morning, even though I had a horrid dream about being chased down tunnels by hamsters with pouches full of Pringles.

CHAPTER SEVEN

The next morning there was still no sign of Gazza. When I first woke up, I thought he'd come back. Fliss was squealing as if he was crawling over her face or something. In fact it was Kenny up to her tricks. She was using Fliss's pony tail to tickle her neck. The first couple of times Fliss just brushed it away, without opening her eyes. Then she must have woken up and remembered the hamster on the loose because she just started to squeal, "AGGHHHH!" After that we were all awake and on the move.

One of the other great things about Rosie's house is the wide staircase. We had mega sleeping-bag races sliding down on our bottoms two at a time. It was excellent until we had to stop because Lyndz split her sleeping bag. She wasn't worried because it was an absolutely ancient one that used to be her brother's. It was already in holes and she was dying for a new one. I'd have been in BIG trouble.

Then we made up a new game for our International Gladiators Challenge. We took it in turns to do a mad dash down the stairs, past the others armed with pillows or squishy poos. (A squishy poo is a sleeping bag filled with clothes for whacking people with.) It was magic!

Adam sat in his chair in the kitchen doorway watching us and bouncing up and down with excitement. We all felt sorry that he couldn't join in and afterwards Lyndz said we should make up some special events that he *could* join in with, which I thought was a neat idea. At least Adam was coming with us to the Pet Show later because, after all, Jenny's really his dog.

We were having such a great time none of us wanted to go home when our parents came to collect us. But we had to because we all needed to get our pets organised.

Gazza still hadn't turned up by the time we left, but Rosie's mum said, "Don't worry we'll keep on searching."

Fliss looked dead miserable. She said there was no point in her going home because she didn't have a pet to get ready. As if we didn't all know that!

Rosie said "You could stay here and help us look for him, if you want to." So that cheered her up a bit.

* * *

When I got home Mum was giving Pepsi a bath, which she hates. She doesn't like water at all. She never jumps in the river like other dogs, she even runs away if Dad turns the hose pipe on in the garden. So I had to hold on to her to keep her in the bath, while Mum shampooed her and then rinsed her off. Then, even though we put the gas fire on and sat her in front of it, she shivered as if she was freezing. Dad rubbed her until she was nearly dry and then I brushed her.

We had to trim some tangled bits of fur from her ears. They do get messy because they hang down in everything. But Dad said, "Never worry. You won't see from a distance."

When we'd finished, she looked so adorable, I told her it didn't matter what the judges thought. I thought she was the most beautiful dog in the world. And I gave her a big hug and she gave me a big lick.

* * *

We'd arranged to meet at the Village Hall
at two o'clock. Brown Owl told us the hall
wouldn't open until two-thirty but we
couldn't wait to get there. I was first
because Mum and Dad dropped me off on
their way to the supermarket. They said
they'd come back later to watch us. It was
starting to rain, but I'd got my kagoul on.

I took Pepsi onto the field behind the
Village Hall for a few minutes and then
she sat down patiently near the entrance,
while we waited for the others. My tummy
was full of butterflies. I was already
feeling excited and now I was starting to
feel a bit nervous so I was glad when
Kenny's dad drove up and dropped her
off.

Kenny was in her Brownie uniform, the
same as me, and she was carrying Merlin
in a brown cardboard box with holes in
the lid. Her dad had made a rope handle
so she could carry it without Merlin

turning somersaults inside. She lifted the lid to show me, but I just took a quick peep and kept my distance. Pepsi was much more interested than I was but we tried to keep her away because whenever she got close to the box we could hear Merlin racing round in circles, scrabbling to get out.

Rosie came next with Fliss. They were walking towards us and Fliss wasn't carrying anything, so Kenny said to me, "Uh-oh, it doesn't look as if Gazza's turned up." But even from a distance we could see she was smiling.

"Have you got him?" I shouted to her.

She frowned at me, as if I'd said something wrong. When she got closer she hissed, "Do you want to tell everyone? It's supposed to be a secret, remember."

Kenny said, "There's nobody here, yet."

"No, but walls have ears," she said. Then she stood close up to us and held her kagoul pocket open. We peeped in and there he was, a bit dusty-looking, but otherwise OK.

"How did you get him out?" whispered Kenny.

"We had to take the floorboard up in the end. It was Adam's idea."

"Where is Adam?"

"Mum's bringing him later. Where's Lyndz?"

But we just shrugged, there was no sign of her yet.

You could tell Jenny and Pepsi were pleased to see each other, their tails were wagging nineteen to the dozen. We would have liked to take them onto the field and let them off their leads but we wanted to keep them nice and clean, so we tried to get them to sit and be good. And they were, until Buster came. Then the trouble started.

Buster isn't used to being on a lead; he was pulling so hard Lyndz couldn't control him. He's only a quarter of the size of Pepsi and Jenny but he's so strong. The minute he saw them he made a bee-line for them. He wouldn't stop fussing and jumping up at them.

"Leave them alone, Buster," Lyndz kept saying. But he wouldn't. He was a menace. Then he noticed Kenny's box and started growling at it. We could hear Merlin scuffling about inside, as if he knew there was an enemy outside, which there was. The minute Lyndz pulled Buster away from Kenny, he started fussing Fliss and getting up on his back legs to reach her pocket.

"Get him off," Fliss squealed.

"I'm trying," said Lyndz, yanking on Buster's lead.

Thank goodness it wasn't long before Brown Owl arrived.

"You girls are very early," she said. "Well, you'd better come inside, out of the rain, but you'll have to wait in the foyer until we're set up. Please keep your pets under control."

"That's what I'm trying to do," said Lyndz, under her breath. But she wasn't having much success.

A few other people were beginning to arrive, so we followed them into the building. But when we got into the foyer and saw who was sitting there, behind a table, ready to take everyone's names, we nearly went home again. It was Snowy Owl, and, in case you've forgotten who Snowy Owl is, she's only Fliss's Auntie Jill. She knew Fliss didn't have her own hamster. Why hadn't we thought about her?

Fliss turned straight round and raced outside, and the rest of us followed her.

CHAPTER EIGHT

"What am I going to do now?" Fliss wailed.

"Look, what are you worried about?" I said. "You haven't done anything wrong."

"Not yet," said Fliss.

"Why not just keep him in your pocket?" said Lyndz. "No one need know."

"Oh, that's all right for you to say, but I was really looking forward to this. I want to be in the Pet Show."

Poor old Fliss, we all wanted her to be in the Pet Show too, but we couldn't think of a way to help. It was raining harder now and we were getting properly wet. But I remembered what my gran always says, where there's a will, there must be a way. I concentrated really hard.

Rosie was standing by Fliss, patting her shoulder. "This is all my fault," she said. "I shouldn't have had that stupid idea in the first place."

"It was a good idea," said Lyndz. "You weren't to know."

"I've got it," I said. "We'll tell Snowy Owl he's Rosie's hamster. She can't take him in because she's got Jenny as well. So you're going to enter him for her."

"Yeah! One-nil!" said Kenny. "Mega-Brain Strikes Again."

"Oh, Frankie, you're so clever," said Rosie.

Mmm, yes, I thought, I am pretty cool, actually.

"OK, let's go," I said. It was nearly two thirty and lots more people were arriving.

But when we went back into the foyer,

we nearly had to come out again, because now there wasn't just Snowy Owl at the desk, her boyfriend, Dishy Dave was there too. Dishy Dave's the caretaker at school. He might recognise Gazza, because he's always in and out of our classroom, checking up on things.

Fliss was about to disappear again, so I grabbed her.

"Just keep him in your pocket," I whispered.

"And try to look natural," whispered Kenny.

Fliss swallowed and gave a big sigh. "I wished I'd stayed at home," she said. But she didn't really, you could tell.

When we got to the front of the queue I went first and gave my name.

"And your dog's?" said Snowy Owl, busy writing.

"Pepsi," I said, smiling.

"What class?" she asked me.

"Class?" I didn't know what she meant.

"Obedience? Appearance? Novelty?"

Well, I knew Pepsi wasn't very obedient so I chose Appearance. Snowy Owl gave me a card with a large number nine on it. "Dogs are in the Main Hall," she said. "Listen for your name to be called."

Rosie chose Obedience as well as Appearance because Jenny's very well-behaved and comes whenever you call her. She got a number ten to hold.

When it came to Lyndz she didn't know which to choose for Buster. He's quite a funny looking thing, not a bit pretty and he certainly doesn't do as he's told.

Snowy Owl told her she'd put him in Obedience because there weren't many dogs in that class, and Novelty too. Buster was number eleven, which made me giggle.

"What's so funny?" said Lyndz.

"You know," I said. "In Bingo, when they call out 'Legs Eleven'. It really suits him." But Lyndz wasn't amused.

Then it was Kenny's turn. "Laura

McKenzie and Merlin," said Kenny.

"And what's Merlin?" asked Snowy Owl, looking at the box.

"My white rat," said Kenny, opening the lid to show her. Snowy Owl went white and leant back in her chair. You could see she wasn't keen on rats. She looked as if she was having trouble swallowing.

"That's alright. I don't need to see him. Just keep him in the box until the judges are ready. Number twelve, room three: small animals."

"Are there any other rats entered?" I asked.

"Not at the moment," said Snowy. "Thank goodness," she added, under her breath.

"So if nobody else comes," said Dave, "you'll win automatically."

That made Kenny grin. Jammy or what!

Then it was Fliss's turn. She was looking very pink. Snowy Owl smiled at her. "I think I know your name," she said.

Well, she ought to, she's her auntie, after all. "Are you just here to keep your friends company?"

Fliss didn't know what to say.

"No," I said for her, "she's entering Rosie's hamster."

Snowy Owl looked at Dave. "Well, I suppose that's allowed."

"Yeah," said Dave. "Why not?" And he winked at us. "We won't tell anyone."

"So, where is he?"

"In her pocket," said Rosie. Snowy Owl frowned.

"Oh, it's OK, he likes it," said Kenny.

"Well, what's his name?"

Fliss looked at Rosie, who looked straight at me. Why do people always expect me to come up with ideas? My mind went to jelly for a second or two, then I suddenly said, "Hammy."

"Hammy the Hamster?" said Dave, not very impressed. But Snowy Owl wrote it down. "Room three, with Kenny. Here's your number."

Fliss looked at the number she was holding out and almost burst into tears. "Sorry about that," said her Auntie Jill. "Luck of the draw, I'm afraid."

We moved away from the table, into the corridor.

"Number Thirteen. Just my luck," said Fliss.

"Well, at least we've got the first bit over," I said. It might have been the first, but it wasn't the worst. That came later.

The door opened. Suddenly we could hear everyone oohing and aahing and making a fuss in the foyer. Who do you think had just walked in? Yes, you've guessed: the dreaded M&Ms. And when we saw Emma Hughes's dog, we nearly all went home.

I'd never seen a dog so white. You almost needed sunglasses to look at her. Rosie, who knows about different kinds of dogs, said she was a husky. Her fur was long and soft and she looked as if she'd had a bath in milk. So this was the famous Duchess of Drumshaw The Third.

You could see straight away she was going to win. Everyone was saying, "Oh, what a beautiful dog! Oh, isn't she absolutely gorgeous." And other sickly things like that. I'm not saying she wasn't a really cute dog, but so are Pepsi and Jenny and no one was making a fuss of them.

Emma Hughes just stood there wearing that *stoopid* face of hers, smiling, as if they were talking about her! When she gave her name in she said, "Which name would you like, her pedigree name or her ordinary, everyday name?"

"What do you usually call her?" Snowy Owl asked.

Then Emma Hughes and Emily Berryman started to giggle. We didn't know what was so funny, until she said. "We call her Snowball." And then she giggled again. Oh, yuk!

"Oh," said Snowy Owl. "That's a good name."

After that she made a big fuss of Emily Berryman's cat. Snowy Owl's a real cat-lover. It was a Siamese, called Smoky. It was so thin it didn't look very well to me. It had this blue ribbon round its neck with a little bell on it and Snowy Owl thought it was lovely.

"OK. Number twenty-one, Emily," she said. "Room two for cats. Go straight along. They'll be starting soon."

We all went off to the rooms we'd been sent to. When those of us with dogs got down to the hall, Brown Owl let us go in, a few at a time. She showed us what we'd have to do, then we had a little practice, before the judges arrived.

It was nearly time for the whole thing to start. I kept looking out for Mum and Dad. I didn't want them to be late and miss seeing me walk Pepsi round in front of the judges. But they came in just before three o'clock. They arrived at the same time as Rosie's mum and Adam.

Adam was dead excited; he kept jiggling in his chair, which got Jenny a bit excited too. Once or twice I noticed Emily Hughes staring at Adam, and I think Rosie did, but she ignored her. I think that's the best thing to do with people like her.

CHAPTER NINE

Just after three o'clock the first people went in with their dogs for the Obedience class. All the parents went in and sat on chairs round the outside of the hall to watch but Brown Owl said I couldn't go in with Pepsi because she might distract the other dogs. I knew she wouldn't, but there was no point arguing with Brown Owl. She was looking a bit stressed out. Instead, I went down the corridor and peeped into the small pets room. They wouldn't let me go in there, either. I suppose they thought

Pepsi might try to eat the small pets or something, so I just hung around the door.

There were lots of little children with hamsters and gerbils and guinea pigs and rabbits, but so far Kenny was the only person who'd brought a rat. She came over to the door to talk to me and she was looking pretty pleased with herself. But then this big boy from the High School wearing a leather jacket pushed past us with a cage with two humungous black rats inside. They made Merlin look like a mouse. Kenny was fed up, but I told her what my gran always says, "It's quality that counts, not quantity."

"Hmmm," she said, not cheered up at all. "I just hope the judges know that."

Fliss was enjoying herself. She was sitting on a chair in the corner with two or three little girls from the Infants, letting them stroke Gazza.

The judges were looking at the rabbits

first; they hadn't started on hamsters yet.

One of the organisers spotted me at the door. She came over, waving her hand for me to go away. "Dogs are in the Main Hall," she said, as if I didn't know, so I went back to the foyer to wait until it was my turn.

There were lots of people waiting outside the hall, including Emma Hughes. Pepsi would have liked to go and get to know her dog, Snowball, but I pulled her away. And then The Goblin came along holding her cat. I was so mad when I saw she was wearing a red rosette on hercollar. On it was a big 1st.

Emma Hughes started squealing and then the two of them stood whispering and giggling together, looking over at me, but I pretended not to notice. Suddenly the hall door opened and out came Buster dragging Lyndz behind him. Lyndz looked really pink and she had the hiccups!

"How did you get on?" I asked.

"D-d-don't ask," Lyndz hiccupped. "He nearly bit the judges."

Just then, Kenny came along, waving a green rosette.

"We won," she squealed. "We came third."

I said, "Fantastic!" And it was. She'd got a rosette, which was what she wanted, but that stuck-up Emma Hughes said, "Third out of three's nothing to brag about."

How did she know there were only three rats? That's another thing about the M&Ms, they seem to know everything that happens. But Rosie and Adam came out next with Jenny who'd won a blue rosette, because she'd come second for good behaviour. So that showed those two!

Lyndz was still hiccupping and Buster was starting to jump up at Kenny's box again.

"Oh— hic— stop it," Lyndz snapped at

him. But he didn't.

"He's a very obedient dog, isn't he?" said Emily Berryman, sarcastically.

Then Buster stopped jumping up and down and turned round and started pulling towards her, just as if he'd heard what she'd said, and wanted to give her a piece of his mind. But I think it was because he'd just caught sight of her cat. And then the trouble really started.

Buster's hackles went up and he was barking so loudly that all four feet lifted off the ground at once. And then, without any warning, he leapt forward, pulling so hard he snapped his lead, which was a pretty old one anyway, and catapulted himself forward to get at the cat. But he missed and landed on Snowball's back. He looked like a little circus dog landing on a horse. It frightened Snowball so much that she leapt sideways, tipping Buster off, and then she panicked and charged out of the foyer, towards the front doors, pulling Emma behind her. Buster was snapping at her heels.

There were lots of people standing near to the door and a lady with a little boy in a buggy was trying to get in, but Snowball was too panicked to wait, so the lady had to. They all collided, Emma tripped over the buggy, the lead slipped through her fingers and in a second Snowball was gone.

Everyone ran after them shouting, "Stop that dog!" and things like that. The next minute we were all outside the building, in the rain, chasing Emma and Lyndz who were trying to catch their dogs. Emily was running, holding onto her cat; I was running with Pepsi; Rosie was running with Jenny; Kenny was running carrying Merlin in his box; even Fliss had joined us by now with Gazza in her pocket.

We were worried at first that the dogs might run out onto the road, but luckily they headed round the side of the building instead and onto the field behind. The faster Snowball ran away, the more determined Buster was to catch her. I don't think he was really interested in Snowball, it was the chase he was enjoying. He was so excited, he'd have chased anything on legs that was running.

They ran right to the bottom of the field, through every puddle on the way. And then they dodged through a hole in the hedge into the sports field and disappeared for a while, although we could hear them both barking their heads off.

Emma and Lyndz were shouting their heads off, too, and so were the rest of us, which Brown Owl told us later was the biggest mistake we made. She said that would have just made them even more excited. And it did. They were wild.

We stopped running when we lost sight of them, but a minute later they popped back through the hedge in a different place and we all started running again.

I don't think we'd ever have caught up with them, if they hadn't turned full circle and headed back towards the Village Hall. But we still weren't quick enough to stop them heading towards the huge pile of coke that was stacked behind the Hall.

"Oh, no! Snowball! Come back!" Emma yelled. But Snowball didn't. She just charged up to it and then raced to the top of it and Buster followed her. The pile of coke collapsed under them and they sank into it, up to their shoulders.

"Snowball! No! No!" It wasn't so much a shout this time, as a wail. By the time Emma reached her, Snowball's coat was covered with coke. And so was Buster's.

Lyndz jumped into the middle and sank down to her knees, but she managed to grab Buster's collar and yank him out with one hand, and grab Snowball with the other one. She pulled them both out.

But when Emma saw the state of her dog, instead of saying thank you to Lyndz, she started screaming at her and telling her it was all her fault. Lyndz tried to say she was sorry, lots of times, but she couldn't finish her sentence.

"It was just an... He didn't really mean... He's quite a nice... dog really."

But Emma Hughes kept interrupting her. Emily Berryman was patting her on the shoulder and trying to calm her down but it wasn't working.

"You did this on purpose," Emma screamed at Lyndz. "You planned this to stop me from winning. You were all in on it."

"No," Lyndz said again. "It was an accident. Honest."

"I don't believe you," she yelled at her. She turned to Emily. "You heard them. They said they'd got something planned, didn't they? They're going to be in real trouble. All of them."

Emily nodded. "Come on," she said. "Let's go and tell Brown Owl."

But instead of going with her, Emma burst out crying. It was awful. We didn't know what to do. We didn't know what to say, either. We just stood there watching her cry in the rain.

The truth is we hadn't had a plan. It was an accident. Lyndz hadn't set Buster onto Snowball, it had been entirely his own idea. Lyndz would have stopped him, if she could. And she did feel bad about it. We all did. The poor dog looked an awful mess. Her feet and legs were splashed with mud and her coat was thick with coke dust. Rosie tried to brush a bit of it off with her hand, but now Snowball's coat was wet, it just smeared everywhere and looked even worse. Jenny and Pepsi sniffed round her sympathetically.

"Get off!" Emma screamed. "Keep away from her." She was nearly in hysterics. "Take those horrible... mutts away."

Mutts! Rosie and I looked at each other and burst out laughing. We tried not to but it just came out. Then Lyndz started and her hiccups came back.

"I think you're all horrible," Emily Berryman said to us and she pulled Emma away and they went back into the Village Hall to find Brown Owl.

"Uh, oh," said Kenny, trying to keep a straight face. "That's put the king in the cake."

"You mean that's put The Queen in the cake," I said. And that set us all off again.

ALL'S WELL THAT ENDS WELL

When we got back in everyone was shouting for us. It seems they'd called out our names for the Appearance class two or three times already. We had to go straight in, even though we were soaking wet and so were the dogs. They didn't look their best, especially Snowball. But it was good fun and in fact, by the end of the afternoon, we'd all won at least one rosette.

Kenny had won her green rosette for coming third with Merlin. Fliss won a special prize for "Hammy" for being the Tamest Hamster in the Show. He was very well behaved and let everyone stroke him. Jenny had already won a blue rosette for coming second in the Most Obedient Dog class and then she won another rosette for being the Dog the Judges Would Most Like to Take Home With Them. Pepsi won a rosette for the Dog With the Most Appealing Eyes. I told you she was cute, didn't I?

And you'll never believe this, but Buster won two!

He won the Most Disobedient Dog in the Show, which just made Lyndz start laughing all over again. Then he won a rosette in Novelty section for walking on his hind legs. It's a pity there wasn't a rosette for the Dog Who Could Jump the Highest, because he'd probably have won that, too.

Emily won a red rosette with her cat and Emma Hughes won two. After Brown

Owl had explained to the judges some of what had happened, and told them how perfect Snowball had looked when she arrived they gave her one rosette for being the Best Groomed Dog in the Show and then one for the Scruffiest Dog in the Show. All in the same afternoon.

Afterwards, we kept wondering when the trouble was going to land, but it never really did. Brown Owl wasn't so cross with us. Snowy Owl had seen how it had all started, so she knew it had been an accident. That was a lucky escape.

Rosie said Adam loved it when she told him the story of what happened out on the field. She had to keep telling him over and over. He was sorry he missed it.

When I told my mum all about it, she said we should try to keep away from the M&Ms for a while, so that's what we're doing. Anyway, since the Pet Show, they seem to be keeping away from us, too.

* * *

So that's the whole story. Come on, we're nearly home, just round this corner. Oh, look! Come on, quick. There's Pepsi, now, at my front gate. I'm so glad she's OK. She looks a bit mucky, though. I wonder who brought her back this time? Uh-oh, there's my mum at the door.

"Francesca, about time! I think you'd better come in and clean up this dog don't you?"

"Coming, Mum."

Oh, well, no rest for the wicked as my gran says. See you again soon. Bye.

The Sleepover Club
at Kenny's

MEET MY SISTER, MOLLY THE MONSTER

CHAPTER ONE

Shall I tell you what I got for Christmas? A pair of shoes with heels. Coo-el. At first my mum said I wasn't old enough for heels.

"I'm ten," I told her. "How old do you have to be?"

Dad said, "You're tall enough already." But he's just worried that one day I'm going to be taller than him.

I really, really wanted them, you know what I mean? So I just kept on and on and in the end... I won! One-nil to me. Yeah!

They've got silver buckles on them. They are drop-dead *gorgeous*. I told Mum and Dad, "You're the best, most groovy parents in the whole wide world." So it was really important to come up with something brill for them.

My dad was easy, I always buy him a big bar of Toblerone. It's his fave chocolate. Then I found the perfect present for Mum: this fat little pig lying down in the mud with all her babies round her. It was so cute. My mum adores pigs, she's got a whole collection. The only trouble was it cost four pounds fifty!

I'm always broke, are you? Kenny is too, money goes through her fingers like water. So we came up with this brilliant idea to earn some, and we got the rest of the Sleepover Club to help us. It was a great plan and we could have been seriously rich, if Kenny's horrible sister, Molly The Monster, hadn't spoiled everything. But don't worry, we got our own back. When we had our last sleepover at Kenny's house we gave her a real scare. It was excellent.

I know, I know, we got grounded again, but listen, it was worth it. She nearly went haywire. And I had the best part in it.

Come on. Let's go up to my room and I'll tell you all about it. But remember, this is Sleepover Club business, so don't tell the others I told you.

Can you remember everyone? Laura McKenzie, otherwise known as Kenny. Fliss – her real name – Felicity Sidebotham. Lyndsey Collins – we call her Lyndz, we've been friends since we first started school. And Rosie Cartwright. And me, of course: Francesca Theresa Thomas, but everyone calls me Frankie.

Now where should I start?

I suppose it really started early in December, the day we were helping our teacher, Mrs Weaver, put up the Christmas decorations in the hall. It was a great skive, it took all afternoon. She kept having to go out to check on the rest of the class so we spent most of the time wrapping ourselves up in paper chains and Chinese lanterns. It was such a laugh. Then we started talking about Christmas presents and what we were going to buy each other. After that I didn't feel like laughing.

"I've got all your presents and they're already wrapped," said Fliss.

I couldn't believe it.

"What've you got us?" said Kenny, straight out, just like that.

"The new Oasis tape." Fliss looked so pleased with herself.

"What, all of us?" said Rosie. "Wowsers!"

The others were dead excited but at first all I could think was: *it's just not fair*. Fliss has so much more money than the rest of us. She gets loads of pocket money. Even Lyndz can earn extra by helping her mum with Spike, their baby, but Rosie and

Kenny and me just get regular pocket money and it's never enough, especially at Christmas. Fliss had spent nearly as much money on each of us as I had to spend on everyone put together.

When I went home I tried to talk to my mum and dad about it but it was a waste of time. My mum and dad are lawyers; they have an answer for everything.

"Please, can I have some extra money? I really need it. Fliss has spent pounds on my Christmas present."

"How do you know that?" said Dad. "Did she leave the price on?"

"Of course not. But everyone knows what tapes cost."

"Well, perhaps Felicity can afford to spend that much on her friends, but it's no reason why you need to," said Mum.

"Remember it's Christmas," said Dad. "It's not a competition."

Well, I knew that. My grandma's always telling me, it's not the gift that counts, it's the thought behind it. But it wasn't just Fliss's present I was worried about. I needed money for everyone's. I went upstairs and emptied my purse and counted my money. But I'd only counted it half an hour earlier and it still only came to £8.43. If I spent £4.50 on my mum's pig I'd have less than £4 to spend on everyone else put together. I wrote a list of the people I wanted to give presents to: Mum & Dad, Grandma, Grandad, Kenny, Fliss, Lyndz, Rosie and some chews for Pepsi, my dog. It just wasn't enough and you didn't have to be Mastermind to work that out.

I needed a good moan, so I got on the phone to Kenny. She's my best friend after all and that's what best friends are for.

"Hiya. It's me, Frankie."

"Oh, hi, Frankie."

"I am so broke. I've only got £8.43 in all the world."

"Well, that's more than I've got."

"I don't know how I can possibly be expected to get all my Christmas presents with a measly £8.43."

"No, nor me."

"And now Fliss has spent pounds on us I feel terrible only spending 50p on her."

"Mmmm. Me too."

This conversation was not helping at all. It was a bit like talking into a black hole. What we needed here was some action.

I said, "So! What are we going to do?"

"Rob a bank?"

"Oh, Kenny, be serious. We need to find some way of making money where we won't end up in jail."

"OK. Let's both make a list. I'll ring you back."

I sat down with a pen and a pad and tried to come up with some ideas, but the more I thought about it the madder I got. There are a few things about my family which I don't think are at all fair. For example, I am an only child, which I think is completely unfair. I keep telling my parents how much I'd like a brother or sister, but they don't take any notice. Although, come to think of it, if I had, it would mean an extra present to buy!

Another thing is that I already do all sorts of jobs which other people could get extra pocket money for, like walking the dog for instance. Yes, I know she's my dog, but even so... And like washing up, or drying and putting away. Other people get extra money for doing that, but I'm expected to do it anyway. Mum and Dad are always telling me, "We're a team, Frankie. We all do our share. That's fair, isn't it?"

I suppose it is, but it doesn't help me make any money, does it? The other thing is, my mum and dad don't give me as much pocket money as other people get, even though they could afford to, because they don't believe in *spoiling* me! Huh! I wish. They think all the adverts on TV make children want lots of things they don't really need, and I suppose they do. But this is different. This is to buy presents for other people, for them even.

But they have an answer to that too. My mum and dad would be happy if I just made them something out of egg boxes, because, yeah, yeah, I know – it's the thought that counts. I just wish all my friends knew that!

At least Kenny did. And, however broke I was, I knew that Kenny was more broke. She's a disaster area where money's concerned.

CHAPTER TWO

Kenny can't earn extra pocket money washing up or drying the pots either, because they've got a dishwasher. She used to be able to earn a bit extra if she loaded it for her mum, but not any more. Last summer they had this big birthday barbecue and Kenny loaded it with paper plates which disintegrated and blocked up the outlet and they had to call a plumber.

"How was I to know?" she said. "They were dead cute plates, with shells and fish on. I thought you'd want to use them again."

"Not much chance of that, now they're sandblasted onto the sides of the dishwasher," her dad yelled at her.

Anyway since then she hasn't been allowed to do any jobs in the kitchen.

Helping out in the garden was another idea, but there's not much to do in December. And Kenny's dad said he had no intention of spring cleaning their garage at this time of year just to please us. So that was that. Back to the drawing board, as my dad says.

"What about washing cars?" Kenny suggested at last.

"That's the first sensible idea you've had," I said. "Whose shall we start on?"

We started on my mum's VW and we were just in the middle of doing it when Lyndz came round on her mountain bike. We're usually dead pleased to see Lyndz but this time we weren't, for obvious reasons.

"Hiya. What're you doing?" she said.

"Crocheting a pair of mittens for the dog!" I said. "What does it look like?"

Lyndz grinned. "Can I help?"

Kenny and I looked down at our feet and sighed. We were both hoping she wouldn't ask that. My mum had agreed to pay Kenny and me 50p each, if we did a good job and didn't leave too much mess. We'd been really sensible and we'd nearly finished, so we didn't want to have to share it with Lyndz. But we both felt really mean leaving her out.

"OK," I said. "But no water fights, or else." I don't know why I even bothered saying that. When Kenny and Lyndz get together they always go bananas. Like that time they had a shopping trolley race in the supermarket and knocked down a humungous stack of bottles of mineral water.

Fortunately, this time Mum didn't go too mad because it was only soapy water they were throwing around and they got most of it over themselves. In fact she gave us all 50p *and* an ice lolly each.

After that we all cycled round to Kenny's house and persuaded her mum to let us clean her Fiesta. And then Kenny's next-door neighbour, Bert, who's really nice, said we could do his. We didn't charge him as much because he's a pensioner. But by the end of the afternoon we'd each made £1.25.

"This is great," said Kenny. "We'll soon be rich."

"How do you make that out?" I said. "My mum won't have her car cleaned again for months." And I knew my dad wouldn't let us loose on his BMW, he's too proud of it.

"We'll ask the other neighbours," she said. "Down your road and in our close."

"What? You mean knock on people's doors?"

"We'll put a note through their letter boxes, like a proper business."

"Are you mad?" I said.

"I think it's a great idea," said Lyndz. So that was it. I was outvoted, which was a bit off since I was the one who'd started it all. But that was only the beginning. On Monday morning, when old Bossyboots Fliss heard about it, she took over straight away.

"Listen, I've got a great idea: we can print the notices out on Frankie's computer," she said, "so we look really professional."

"We?" I said. "Since when did you need to earn any money? You're loaded already."

"Well, I'm not," said Rosie. "I could do with earning some money before Christmas. Adam wants a new game for his computer and I said I'd give Tiff something towards it." Adam is Rosie's brother, he's computer-mad. And Tiff is Rosie's older sister. She's fifteen and she works after school in the local supermarket, so she could afford it on her own really.

"Listen," said Kenny. "If we do it together and get properly organised, we'll be much quicker, so we'll do more cars, so we'll earn more money, so there'll be enough for all of us."

"Yeah," said Lyndz. "And it'll be more fun, if it's all five of us."

I nodded. I supposed she was right. But I had a funny feeling that things were already getting out of hand. It felt like another of those times when, as my gran says, it would all end in tears.

After school everyone came round to my house and we went up to my bedroom. I'm not supposed to have friends round after school, I'm supposed to go next door to Auntie Joan's until my mum and dad get home from work, and watch TV with the gruesome Nathan. He's not my cousin, thank goodness. And Joan's not my real auntie, I just call her that. But she's a good sport and she said that just this once we could go up and play on my computer, and she'd look in on us and bring us some cookies, when they came out of the oven.

"You're the best," I said and gave her a hug.

"Make sure you're sensible," she warned us and she gave me our front door key.

We threw our coats on my bed and I turned on my computer.

"OK. What shall we call ourselves?" said Fliss.

"Call ourselves?"

"Yeah. You need a catchy name, so people remember it."

"What about, *Sleepover Club Car Wash*," said Lyndz.

"That's no good," said Kenny. "It sounds as if we'll be going to sleep on the job."

"I know," said Fliss, "A1 Car Cleaners. That way we'll get to be first in the phone book. Andy told me lots of businesses do that." Andy is sort of Fliss's step-dad and he's a plumber so I suppose he should know.

"Get a life," I said. "We're never going to get in the phone book."

"We've got to think big," said Kenny. But even she could see that was a *stoopid* idea.

In the end, we called ourselves: Five Star Car Wash which was much better, because there are five of us and five star means the best. You can probably guess whose idea that was! No, it wasn't Fliss's, actually. It was mine, thank you very much.

This is what our notice looked like:

★ ★ ★ ★ ★

Five Star Car Wash
On your own doorstep!
We'll bring our own bucket and sponge

☺

**ONLY £1.50 PER CAR.
FRANKIE THOMAS:
17 THE RIDGEWAY !**

☆ ☆ ☆ ☆ ☆

At first we couldn't agree how much we should charge. We finally settled on £1.50, which seemed a lot, but we had to share it between five. Still, as Kenny had said, we'd be able to clean more cars so we'd earn more in the long run.

Then we printed off half the notices for Kenny's close, with her name and address on the bottom and the other half for my road with my name on the bottom.

"We can start on Fliss's street later," I said.

"If we're not too busy," said Kenny.

We were really excited. Before they left, everyone helped me post the notices through all the doors in my road. We rushed to get them done, before my mum and dad came home.

I know! You needn't look like that. I wasn't going to keep it a secret forever; I did intend telling them. I just thought I'd wait for the right moment... when they were both in a good mood... tomorrow, perhaps… or the next day.

And it wasn't easy, not to tell them, because that night I was nearly bursting to. I lay in bed planning all the things I'd buy when I was rich. And I probably would have been, if Molly the Monster hadn't stuck her nose in where it didn't belong.

CHAPTER THREE

Have I told you before about Kenny's sister Molly? She's gruesome. Poor old Kenny has to share a bedroom with her and she hates it. It's not a very big room and there are two beds in it with a dressing table between them. There isn't even room for a wardrobe, that's out on the landing. Molly is so bossy she's always making rules about what Kenny can and can't do in her own bedroom.

For example, Kenny has a pet rat, called Merlin. He has to live in the garage. Molly won't allow her to have him in the bedroom. Kenny has to go outside if she wants to play with him.

The other thing she does is to draw a line with chalk down the middle of the dressing table and if anything of Kenny's slides over onto her side she throws it away! I mean it. That's really hard for Kenny, because she's a bit untidy at the best of times. She's always finding her things chucked in the waste basket. All Molly says is, "Well, you'd better keep them on your own side, then, hadn't you?" Honestly!

Kenny and Molly have always fallen out, ever since Kenny was little. She's almost lost count of the horrible things Molly has done. Once, when they were on holiday, she pushed Kenny out of bed and nearly broke her arm. And another time, when Kenny was really small, Molly cut off her hair, all of it, except a little sprout which stuck out at the front. Kenny's still got a photo of it. She looks like a Cabbage Patch doll.

And then the worst time was when their dad was digging a pond in the garden; while he was mixing the cement to lay the base, Molly buried all Kenny's Playpeople in the hole. She only told her after the pond was finished and filled with water and it had fish in it. That's what she's like, gruesome with a capital GRRR!

Molly hates it when we have a sleepover at their house, because she has to move out and sleep on the camp bed in Emma's room. Emma is their other sister, she's sixteen, which is the reason she has a room to herself while Kenny and Molly have to share. So, whenever we sleepover at Kenny's, we can't get rid of Molly. She hangs around, telling us all the things we're not allowed to do, like touching her jewellery, as if we'd want to, or getting on her bed with our shoes on, as if we would, and *looking at* her make-up.

"How does looking at it wear it out?" I said.

Kenny pulled a being sick face. "*She* certainly needs make-up," she said. "She could do with a complete mask."

"I heard that," said Molly. She was hiding behind the door. That's the other thing, she's always ear-wigging on our conversations and it really gets on our nerves.

But sometimes Kenny gets her own back. Molly's twelve and she's got one or two tiny spots starting. She peers at them in the mirror so Kenny tells her how they're getting bigger and one day they'll cover her whole face. Last time we were there we made this mixture of salt and pepper in water and told her it was a secret recipe Lyndz's grandma had given her for spot lotion and we'd made it specially for her.

"I haven't got spots," she shrieked. "I

have not got spots!" She nearly went ballistic!

We hadn't had a sleepover at Kenny's for ages, because of Molly. Poor old Kenny's tried complaining to her mum and dad but they always say the same thing. Kenny knows it off by heart: "We've only got three bedrooms. Emma's the oldest; she's got GCSEs this year; she needs a room of her own to study in. Anyway, we both shared bedrooms with our brothers and sisters when we were your age. It's good for you to share."

"Good for me?" Kenny screamed at us. "How can it be good for me? I'll be lucky if I live to be twelve. I'd rather sleep out in the garage with Merlin."

"Why don't your family move?" said Rosie. "Get a bigger house."

"We've been trying to for ages, but we can't find one Mum likes. Dad doesn't care; he's never there." Kenny's dad's a doctor, he works all the time. "But Mum is so fussy.

The house has got to be exactly what she wants and it never is."

Kenny was telling us about it while we were waiting for netball practice. She was even more steamed up than usual with Molly because that morning she'd found her *Girl Talk* comic screwed up in the waste basket and she'd only read half of it.

"How was I to know?" said Molly. "It was on the floor. You should put your things away."

"I'd flatten her," I said.

"*You* probably could," said Kenny. "But she's bigger than me."

"Why don't you tell your mum and dad?" asked Fliss.

"I already did, but what's the point? They don't do anything."

"I thought you had a caravan," said Rosie. "Why not ask if you can sleep in that?"

Everyone went quiet and looked at their feet. "It's haunted," said Kenny.

"Haunted?"

Kenny nodded. "Poltergeist."

Rosie's eyes nearly popped out of her head, but Kenny didn't want to get started on that story. None of us like that story, it's too creepy. So we got back to the important subject.

"Anyway," said Kenny, "it's my turn for you all to sleepover at my house next, so we need to start thinking of some juicy revenges for Monster-face. Anybody got any good ideas?"

Ideas? We had loads. It was pay back time for Molly The Monster and we were really looking forward to it.

CHAPTER FOUR

But before I tell you about that, let's get back to the car wash business, which was not going too well. Before we even had a chance to get started my mum and dad found out what we were up to and they were not pleased. It was Auntie Joan's fault.

On Tuesday and Wednesday, when I got in from school, I kept waiting for our first customer to ring or knock on the door. Kenny was phoning every five minutes to check whether I'd heard anything, because she still hadn't, so I had to tell her to get off the phone in case anyone was trying to ring us. But there was nothing. Not a sausage.

Then, on Wednesday night, Mum and Dad saw the notice. They were having a cup of coffee in Auntie Joan's kitchen and they saw it stuck on her notice board.

"*Five Star Car Wash*! What's all that about?"

"Frankie!"

Thank goodness they didn't go *too* mad. They just had a medium-sized wobbly. But they said I should have told them first; then they could have saved me the trouble of doing the notices. Which they said were very good. But, grrrrr, they still wouldn't let me do it. And shall I tell you why? Because I wasn't *old enough*. I'm never old enough for anything, according to them.

"The law's quite clear about it," said Dad. "Children under thirteen are not allowed to do paid work, so that's that."

"But all my friends do," I said. "*Other people* get extra pocket money for picking the newspaper up off the floor."

"Pocket money's different," said Mum. "Parents can give as much or as little pocket money as they like. We're talking about people outside the family paying children to work. It's against the law."

"But it's only car washing," I said. "Everybody does it."

"Not lawyers' daughters," said Mum.

"Especially this lawyer's daughter," said Dad. "Case closed. No room for appeal."

So, I was right, wasn't I? I knew if I told them, they'd say no. I guess that's why Kenny didn't tell her mum and dad either. But they still found out – thanks to Molly.

Monster-face is in the same class at school as Howard Jinks. He's a boy who lives down their road. He's gross. He's always thumping people. He took one of our notices into school and showed it to people in their class. Then everyone started calling Molly 'Five Star Car Wash' all day, and asking her where her bucket and sponge were. When she came home she was fizzing like an unexploded bomb.

She stuffed the note in Kenny's face. "If this is your idea of a joke, it isn't funny."

"It wasn't meant to be funny. We were trying to earn some money, that's all."

"Well, you can forget it," said Molly. "You're in big trouble." And she rushed into the kitchen, yelling her head off, to find their mum.

Kenny's mum was cross because she was in the middle of cutting someone's hair at the time. Kenny's mum does some hairdressing at home and she said Molly had shown her up in front of the lady. So she got a good telling off, hah! But later, when their dad came home and saw the notice, they both gave Kenny a *serious talking to*.

They said she definitely should have asked their permission; which Kenny knew. They said she certainly shouldn't have been wandering up and down the street, knocking on people's doors, because it wasn't safe to do that nowadays. Kenny told them we hadn't knocked on any doors, we'd just posted our notices through the letter boxes. And they said, she wasn't anything like old enough (yawn, yawn) to be washing other people's cars, it was too much responsibility. If she did any damage they'd have to pay the bill. Kenny tried to point out that you can't do much damage with a sponge and a plastic bucket, but they said that wasn't the point.

But the good news was they didn't actually say she couldn't do it! They said *if* anyone answered the advert and, *if* it was someone they knew, they'd think about it.

That was when Molly the Bomb exploded. "Is that it!" she yelled. "Is she going to get away with this? Are you going to let her off as easy as that? I don't believe this!"

"It's nothing to do with you," said Kenny. "Mind your own business."

"This is my business. If you go showing me up at school, it's my business."

"Oh, go and boil your head," said Kenny.

But after that Molly was even more horrible to her and did everything she could to get Kenny into trouble and instead of just having a chalk line down the middle of the dressing table, she used a piece of rope to divide the room up and said Kenny couldn't even step in her half of the room which is stupid because Molly's got the door in her half.

"I'm sick of you," Kenny told her.

"So what are you going to do about it?" said Molly, lounging on her bed.

"I'm going to fix you. You just wait."

"Oh, yeah. You and whose army?"

"Me and my Sleepover Club army," thought Kenny. But she didn't say anything. She thought she'd keep that as a surprise.

"I hate my sister," she told us the next morning on the way to school. "I'm going to sue her. Frankie, will you ask your mum and dad how I do it?"

"I don't think you can sue your sister just for being gruesome," I told her.

"Well, you ought to be able to. She's going to be a criminal when she grows up and I'm sick of her practising on me."

"So what are you going to do?" said Rosie.

"I don't know. Yet."

"Have you asked your mum and dad about the sleepover?" said Fliss.

Kenny sighed again. "They said it's too close to Christmas, but I'm not giving up."

Have you noticed how unfair it is around Christmas? I don't know about your parents, but mine are always going out to parties with their friends, eating vol-au-vents and sausage rolls and having a great time, but the minute I ask to have a party, or have my friends round, they go on about how busy they are. And Kenny's parents are just the same.

There was only one weekend left before

Christmas. We couldn't bear to wait until after the holidays. Kenny begged her mum and dad on bended knees, pretty please, the whole works. No luck. So then she promised them all sorts of things, if they'd let her: she'd tidy her bedroom, stop biting her nails, even eat cabbage. When that didn't work either, she threatened to run away. The trouble is Kenny's done that loads of times. When she was little, every time she fell out with Molly, she used to write a note for her mum to say she was running away, then she'd just sneak upstairs and hide under her bed. So now her mum knows exactly where to find her.

In the end Kenny was so desperate she did a really big thing. She told us it was the *ultimate sacrifice* and she was prepared to make it, for the Sleepover Club. That's the kind of person Kenny is. That's why she's my all-time best friend.

She agreed to wear a dress on Christmas Day. Oh, you may think that's nothing, because I bet you wear dresses or skirts all the time, but it was really big for Kenny. Kenny lives and dies in her Leicester City football strip. Her mum tries everything to get her out of it, for at least one day a year. So she was really pleased. In fact, you'd have thought Kenny had given her a present.

Kenny had to promise in front of the whole family *and* sign a piece of paper. But she did it. The sleepover was settled for Saturday night. And Molly was *furious!*

"You mean to say I've got to give up my bed for those little gonks. It's not fair. I never have friends round to stay."

"That's because you haven't got any friends," said Kenny.

"I have too. Anyway, how come she gets everything she wants? She's so spoiled. I won't do it. I won't! You can't make me."

But they did. Hee-hee-hee-hee-hee! One-nil to Kenny!

CHAPTER FIVE

Kenny couldn't wait for school the next morning. She came rushing to find us with the good news. She was late because she'd been to the dentist with her mum. The rest of us were already in the hall, rehearsing for the Christmas Concert. Well, actually we were waiting for Mrs Weaver to get round to our part, so we were at the back of the hall, supposed to be practising our lines.

"OK," she said. "The sleepover's on Saturday night. So it's PBT for Monster-face."

"PBT?" said Fliss.

"Pay back time for Molly," I said. Sometimes she's so slow.

"Oh, yeah," said Fliss.

"Let's start planning it," said Rosie.

"Someone slip back to the classroom and get a notebook," said Fliss.

I said, "What did your last servant die of?"

"I'll go," said Lyndz. Lyndz likes to keep the peace.

It didn't matter about practising because we all knew our lines back to front and standing on our heads. No, I mean it. We'd been practising handstands at the back of the hall and reciting our lines at the same time, because it was boring, just waiting around. Mrs Weaver didn't seem to mind as long as we kept quiet. She'd been rehearsing Alana Palmer and Regina Hill for over half an hour.

Alana Palmer couldn't remember any of her lines and Regina Hill kept changing hers. Regina Hill's this weird new girl who's just started in our class. She's even taller than me. And she's so stuck up. She's nearly as bad as the M&Ms, our worst enemies. She even argues with the teacher. She was just making her lines up as she went along and they were different every time, so Alana never knew when to come in.

Between them they were driving Mrs Weaver mad, but at least it gave us time to plan our sleepover. Lyndz handed the notebook to me. I always have to do the writing.

"We could make Molly an apple pie bed," said Rosie. "After we've used the bed for the sleepover, of course. Before we go home."

"Won't that make a terrible mess?" said Fliss. "My mum'd have a fit."

"You don't use apple pies, dumbo," I said.

"We just make the bed so Molly can't get into it," said Kenny.

"What for?" said Fliss.

"To annoy her, of course."

Fliss rolled her eyes; she still couldn't see the point.

"Well, you come up with something better, then," I said.

"We could make some fairy cakes with plastic flies in them," said Lyndz suddenly.

"Yeah, great," said Rosie. "But where will we get the flies?"

"Joke shop," said Lyndz. "I've seen them."

"We could use real flies," said Kenny. "And spiders..."

"And slugs," I said. "And worms..."

"And woodlice..."

"Oh, gross," said Rosie.

"Great," said Kenny.

"I don't know," said Fliss. "Flies carry germs. I would have thought you'd have known that, Kenny."

"I do know it. I still think it's a good idea."

"Better stick to plastic," said Rosie.

"What about the spot mixture?" said Lyndz. "That really got her going."

"Yeah, but we've done that. We need something new. Something seriously nasty."

The trouble is we knew the really nasty things we'd like to have done would get us into big trouble. Like the time we drew five moustaches on Molly's poster of the Spice Girls. They looked so funny, we nearly died laughing, but she didn't; she went into orbit. We got a real telling off *and* we had to club together to buy her a new poster.

We needed to think of things where we wouldn't leave any evidence behind us. Things where it would be her word against ours. Even better, things where she wouldn't even know for sure it was us. Hmmm. It needed some thinking about. And we'd only got two days before the sleepover.

We didn't have another chance to work on our list that day because, when we went back to the classroom, Mrs Weaver worked us twice as hard as usual to make up for all the time we'd spent not doing our work when we were in the hall. As if the Christmas Concert was our idea!

At lunchtime, when we might have had time, we got into this argument about when we should give each other our Christmas presents. I hadn't bought mine yet. I was still hoping to earn some more money. I knew I couldn't do any car washing in our road; my mum and dad had put their foot down about that. But if Kenny's mum and dad let her do some in their close I could help. She hadn't heard a thing from any of the neighbours yet, which I thought was a bit strange, but we were still hopeful. So I wanted us to swop presents on the last day of term which would give us nearly a week more.

"But it's our last sleepover before Christmas," said Fliss, whingeing again.

"Well? It doesn't have to be *then*," I said.

"But why not?"

"I haven't bought all your presents yet."
The real truth was, I hadn't bought any.

"You can get them on Saturday, before you come."

"Yeah, that's what I'm going to do," said Rosie.

Kenny and I didn't want to admit we hadn't even got the money to get them then.

"I might not have time, anyway," said Kenny. "I shall be busy getting ready." The others all looked at her. "Tidying up and things."

Even I had to laugh. Kenny doesn't know the meaning of tidying up.

"It would be more special," said Rosie, "to swap presents at the sleepover."

"Let's vote on it," said Fliss, bossing again.

Three against two. We were outvoted. So that was how it was left. We just crossed our fingers, hoping that someone in Kenny's close would book a carwash before Saturday.

Kenny did everything she could. All week she'd been smiling and waving to the neighbours, trying to be nice and polite. One or two of them had given her these funny embarrassed smiles and sort of shaken their heads. It was Saturday morning before she found out why. She met Bert's wife coming out of her gate next door.

"You tell your mum and dad they didn't need to send Molly round to apologise, my duck. We thought it was a clever idea of yours, trying to raise some money. We weren't in the least bit offended. It's a shame they won't let you do it."

Kenny couldn't believe her ears. No wonder no one in the close had rung her up. Molly had been round to every house and collected up the notices and told the neighbours that Kenny wasn't allowed to wash their cars and that their mum and dad had sent *her* round to apologise about Kenny being such a nuisance! And, then, as if that wasn't bad enough, the horrible toad had torn our notices up into hundreds of pieces and flushed them down the toilet. When we found out we'd have liked to flush her down the toilet.

Kenny rang to tell me all about it. "Frankie, don't speak. Don't say a word. You're never going to believe this. My sister is unbelievable!"

Afterwards we were both fizzing mad. Now she'd gone too far.

"This means war," said Kenny. "I'll see you later, Frankie."

"Yeah. See you," I said. Which I knew sounded pretty feeble but I couldn't think what else to say. I was still in shock. And when I put down the phone I realised I was still too broke to buy any presents and now my last chance had gone and I'd have to go to the sleepover without any.

CHAPTER SIX

Kenny had told us to arrive for the sleepover at about four o'clock. She'd persuaded her mum to let us come early because we wanted to get started on the *cooking*. You know... the plastic fly cakes! Kenny's mum's really good like that, she often lets us do some cooking. Usually she stays and does it with us, but this time we needed to be on our own.

Kenny had persuaded her we could make fairy cakes with our eyes closed; we'd made them loads of times at school.

So she'd put all the ingredients out on the worktop for us and said we could call out if we needed her. We dumped our bags in Kenny's room and raced down to the kitchen and put aprons on.

The house was full, because everyone was in, even Kenny's dad was at home for once. He was sitting in the lounge watching the football. Emma had a friend round and they were up in the bathroom, dyeing Emma's hair. Kenny's mum was wrapping Christmas presents on the dining-room table and Molly was helping her. So we had the kitchen to ourselves, at least for the moment.

Kenny closed the kitchen door and said, "OK. Let's do this really quickly before anyone comes in. Frankie, you put the paper cases in the tin. Fliss, you whisk these eggs. Lyndz, turn the oven on. Rosie, weigh out the currants."

Rosie started to grin. "The plastic flies, you mean."

We all bit our lips to stop us from giggling. We didn't want Lyndz to start hiccuping because we knew there'd be no stopping her and we needed to get on.

Kenny put all the ingredients in the bowl and beat the mixture so hard it flew up in the air. When her arm started to ache she passed it round and we all had a go. It wasn't a Christmas cake, but we all had a wish anyway. We didn't tell each other what we'd wished for, but we could tell by the soppy grin on Fliss's face what her wish was about. She wants to marry Ryan Scott, who is a really *stoopid* boy in our class. I despair of her sometimes.

Then we all crowded round while Rosie poured the currants in.

"Who's got the *you-know-whats*?" whispered Kenny.

Lyndz took a plastic bag out of her tracksuit pocket. She emptied it out on the worktop. Two plastic spiders fell out.

"They're not flies," hissed Kenny.

"They'd sold out of flies," said Lyndz. "That's all they'd got."

"They're miles too big," yelled Kenny.

"Shhh," I said, terrified her mum would come in. "We'll cut the legs off. Where does your mum keep her scissors?"

Kenny was still giving Lyndz a hard stare, so I went to a drawer and found a pair of scissors. They were pretty big but they would hardly cut butter. I could probably have chewed the legs off quicker. Kenny plopped a dollop of mixture in each of the paper cases and then I pushed the two plastic spiders into the mixture.

"This is never going to work," said Kenny. "They'll probably climb to the top when they're cooking and give the game away."

"They're not climbing anywhere," I said, "with no legs!" But, just in case, I gave the cakes another poke with my finger. Then I scraped round the bowl to get a bit more mixture and heaped the two cake cases higher. Kenny was just about to put the tray in the oven when Rosie said, "Shouldn't we mark them, then we'll know which ones the spiders are in?"

"Good thinking, Batman," I said. "What shall we use?"

"We could put a cherry on those two," said Fliss. "If your mum's got any."

"That's no good," said Kenny. "Molly hates cherries. She'd never eat them."

"That's even better," I said. "We'll put cherries on all the others."

"Mega-brain strikes again," said Kenny, darting into the pantry and coming back with a tub of cherries. She stuck one on each of them, apart from the *special* ones. Thank goodness we'd put them in the oven and disposed of the leftover legs, and started to clear up, before Kenny's dad put his face round the door.

"Mmmm, something smells good. Any chance of a cuppa?" he said.

"Okay," said Kenny. "We'll do it in a minute."

"No hurry. In fact, I'm happy to wait till the cakes are ready."

When they came out of the oven they looked and smelt scrummy. The good news was the spiders hadn't climbed to the top. The bad news was Kenny hadn't pressed the cherries down hard enough and two or three had fallen off. So then we had a bit of an argument about which ones they'd fallen off and whether we could still be sure which were the *special* ones. Luckily, thanks to my idea of putting an extra spoonful of mixture on top, the special cakes were noticeably bigger.

Kenny made a cup of tea for her mum and dad, while I arranged the cakes on a plate. We put Molly's on a small Peter Rabbit plate, and Lyndz poured a glass of orange juice, specially for her, with some salt and pepper in it!

By the time we took them through, Kenny's mum had finished wrapping presents and Molly was sitting on the sofa watching the end of the match with her dad. Kenny gave them their drinks. We all crowded into the lounge and I offered the cake plate to her mum. And then disaster struck.

Before I could offer her dad one, he helped himself to one off Molly's plate.

"You can't eat that," said Kenny, as if it was about to bite him. "It's Molly's," she added quickly. "She doesn't like cherries. We made two without, specially for her. "

"That's OK," Molly said, handing him the plate. "You can have them both. I wouldn't touch them anyway, knowing who made them." And she gave Kenny a horrible look.

"Never mind, peanut," said her dad, winking at Kenny. "All the more for me." And he took the plate and bit into one.

"What the...." but he never finished his sentence because he must have bitten hard into one of the spiders and cracked a filling. He nearly went ballistic.

Uh-oh. We really thought we were in for it. We all went so red that we looked like a bad case of sunburn, especially Fliss. But no one noticed. They were all more concerned with Kenny's dad and what he could do about his tooth.

"This is so typical. Why do these things have to happen on a Saturday afternoon? And so close to Christmas. When am I going to get it fixed in the next few days?"

"I don't understand how you can crack a filling on a fairy cake," said her mum.

Fortunately, just then Emma and her friend Hayley raced down to see what had happened and Emma dripped hair dye on the carpet so there was even more fuss about that. And then the football match finished in a draw. Big tragedy! Apparently it was a match Leicester needed to win and Kenny's dad said that was the final straw. He sank back on the sofa, clutching his head. Even Kenny started behaving as if there'd been a national disaster.

I looked at Rosie, who isn't interested in football either, and we rolled our eyes to the ceiling. But then she kept on giving me funny looks until I noticed what she was looking at – the plate with the two cakes. It was still sitting there on the arm of the sofa. While everyone was making a fuss, I picked it up and slipped into the kitchen and tipped them both into the bin.

When I came back Kenny's dad was saying again, "Why do things like this always have to happen when I'm on call?"

"I don't see what difference that makes," said her mum.

"Well, I could have rung Herman. He might have done a quick repair for me. He owes me a favour." Herman was a good friend of Kenny's dad's, as well as being his dentist.

"Oh, Jim, why don't you ring him? It's worth a try."

So, even though it was Saturday teatime, the dentist told him to come right over.

Kenny's dad got his coat on and hunted for his car keys. We were just beginning to relax and think we'd got away with it, when he came back in and said, "I'd like to know what you girls put in those cakes. It felt like biting on a bullet."

Kenny looked as if she might burst, she was so red, but her mum said, "Now, Jim, don't go blaming the girls. There was nothing wrong with my cake; it was delicious. You know what your teeth are like: if there's one seed left in a currant you'll be the one to find it. You've had that filling replaced twice before."

"All the same I might just take it along as evidence," he said, looking round for it.

"Oh, get off with you," said her mum. And lucky for us he did.

It was a good job I'd disposed of the evidence, because Monster-face was watching us all, as if she suspected something was going on. So, to throw her off the scent, we sat down and scoffed the rest of the cakes. "Mmmm, they're so light," I said.

"And soft," agreed Kenny.

"They melt in your mouth," said Rosie.

"Scrummy," said Lyndz. "Sure you don't want the last one?" she asked Molly.

Molly screwed up her nose as an answer. She still hadn't touched her drink either.

"You don't know what you're missing," I said, finishing the last one.

"You'd think we were trying to poison you," said Kenny. And after that we couldn't keep our faces straight. We just raced off upstairs to Kenny's bedroom and collapsed on her bed. But there was no chance to talk about anything, because guess who followed us!

CHAPTER SEVEN

Molly stood in the doorway, glaring at us. "Remember, half of this room is mine and you're not to touch anything."

"Yeah, yeah, you already told us fifty times before," said Kenny and she got up and closed the door on her. For a change Molly didn't open it and start up again.

We were dying to talk about what had happened, but we knew she'd be standing outside ear-wigging. So Kenny got up and put on her cassette player really loud and we huddled together on her bed and whispered.

"That was a lucky escape," I said. "It's a good job Rosie spotted the cakes."

"And you got rid of the evidence," said Rosie.

"I feel really bad about my dad," said Kenny.

Lyndz said, "Yeah, so do I." In fact we all did. None of us liked going to the dentist.

"And we still haven't got our revenge on you-know-who." Kenny pointed to the door.

Somehow making an apple pie bed in the morning seemed a pathetic idea. But later on we came up with a much better one. I'll tell you how it happened.

About half-past six Kenny's mum called us down for tea. She'd made us vegetable lasagne which was *de-licious*. Fortunately Molly the Monster didn't eat with us, because she'd taken herself off to bed. She *said* she felt ill. Well, she couldn't blame it on our cakes because she hadn't touched them or her orange juice. She didn't really look ill. Kenny said it was just an excuse to have their mum running up and down-stairs after her.

Emma and her friend Hayley were going to cook for themselves later on. They were making chicken masala, which I didn't fancy in the least, but then I'm a vegetarian, but the afters, hot fudge bananas, looked scrummy. They said they *might* save us some, if we kept out of their way.

While we were still eating there was a phone call from Kenny's dad to say he'd got his tooth fixed and he was going to stay a bit longer and have a cup of coffee with Herman. Then about half an hour later there was another call to say he'd been bleeped so he was going on now to see a patient and he'd be home later.

After we'd finished eating we carried the dishes through to the kitchen. Kenny's mum loaded them into the dishwasher and then sent us through to the lounge because Emma and Hayley were already starting their cooking and it isn't a very big kitchen.

Over the back of a chair in the lounge was one of the hairdressing gowns Kenny's mum uses, so I just threw it over my head and crept up behind Fliss, pretending to be a ghost, and gave her the fright of her life. And that was how we got the idea.

"That's it, that's it," Kenny started to squeal. Then she lowered her voice. "Come on, let's go upstairs." We all scooted up to her room where she outlined her plan. It was ace. We were so excited we were hopping around the bedroom rubbing our hands.

Suddenly we heard the phone ring. It was Kenny's dad again. This definitely wasn't his day. Now his car had broken down. He'd already been to see his patient, but he was stuck and couldn't get home. Kenny's mum came into the bedroom looking really flustered.

"Listen, girls, I'm going to have to go and pick up Kenny's dad. Do you think you'll be OK with Emma and Hayley, while I'm gone?"

"Course we will," said Kenny. Emma often babysits for her and Molly.

"Well, I don't like leaving you all with Emma, and I wouldn't normally do it, but today hasn't exactly been a normal day. I won't be gone long."

"Don't worry about it," said Kenny. It was good news for us. Now we'd be able to creep in and scare Molly more easily, with both her parents out of the way. "Hang loose, Mother Goose," she said. "In fact, if you like we'll get ready for bed now."

That was a bit of a mistake because it made her mum suspicious. After all it was still only eight o'clock. "You're not going to make a lot of noise, are you, Laura, because Molly isn't very well and she's trying to rest."

"She looked all right to me," said Kenny. "She's faking, you know. It's just to get attention. You shouldn't give in to her."

Kenny's mum smiled and said, "Just try not to make too much noise and disturb her, all right?"

Kenny pulled a face, but nodded. It was perfect – her mum and dad would be out of the house; Emma and Hayley were busy downstairs in the kitchen; Molly was already in bed. We waited, as quiet as mice, in Kenny's room until we heard her mum's car start up and move off down the road.

"OK, let's get going," said Kenny.

"Who's going to do it?" I said. Everybody looked at me as if I'd asked a really stupid question. "Why me?"

"Because you're the biggest," said Kenny.

"So?"

"You look the most like a fully grown ghost," Rosie agreed.

"What's a fully grown ghost when it's at home?" I said.

"You know what she means," said Fliss.

I didn't, but there was no point arguing because I was outvoted, four to one. I wasn't sure it was such a good idea any more, but the others were all for it. It was

OK for them; they didn't have to do it.

I slipped the hairdressing gown over my head. Then Kenny poked about under her bed and found me a set of those long plastic finger nails. I put my hands under the gown and then Kenny fitted them onto the ends of my fingers. They looked really drastic.

The trouble started when we lifted the gown up to cover my face, I couldn't see a thing. As soon as I tried to move I walked into Kenny's bed.

"Ow! This is useless. I'll probably fall downstairs and break my neck," I yelled.

"Shhh!" said Kenny. "She'll hear you. Wait a minute. Take it off and I'll cut two eye holes in it."

Well, that was a real performance because the first time she cut them too close together and I still couldn't see a thing, so she had to cut a second set.

"Won't your mum hit the roof, when she sees what you've done?" said Fliss.

"She's got lots of these gowns. I'll get rid of this one. She'll never miss it."

At last we'd got two eye holes that I could just about see through. And then I had a little practice walking round the room in the dark. Kenny turned her light out and pulled back the curtains so a bit of light from the street lamps came through. The others said I looked dead creepy and I started to make sort of ghostly noises, until Fliss really started to freak.

"OK, that's enough practising," said Kenny. "Let's do it."

"Do what?" I said from under the cape. "What am I supposed to do?"

"Go in there and give her the scare of her life."

"What if I wake her up?"

"You'll have to wake her up or there's no point doing it," said Kenny.

"But what if she jumps out of bed and catches me?"

"As soon as she's awake you'll have to leg

71

it back to my room. Now, come on."

Kenny opened her bedroom door and listened. There was no sound from downstairs. The kitchen door was closed, so she pushed me forwards along the landing as far as Emma's bedroom door. It was closed too and I hadn't got a hand free, what with the gown and the finger nails, so Kenny bobbed in front of me, turned the door handle and opened the door. It made a loud creaking noise and I could hear Fliss gasp. I was ready to forget the whole thing too, but Kenny gave me another push and I ended up in the room.

It took ages for my eyes to get used to the dark and I walked into the end of the camp bed, trying to make out where Molly was. Fortunately she wasn't in it. She was in Emma's bed. I shuffled over to her and stood looking down on her and then I didn't know what to do next.

I knew the others were outside the room listening, so I thought about doing a few ghostly moans, but I was frightened of waking Molly up in case she caught me before I had a chance to scarper. Kenny had said just blow on her, but how could I do that with this rotten cape over my face. So, instead, I waved my hands about a bit to make a draught. I felt really stupid. And scared.

Suddenly something terrible happened. Molly's eyes opened and she stared right at me. I nearly died. I couldn't move. I was just glued to the spot. I felt as if I would never move again, until she screamed. I soon moved then.

She just screamed and screamed and screamed. It was deafening. I don't remember how I got along the landing. I ran straight into the others who were still crowding round outside the door. The next moment we'd fallen into Kenny's room, pushed the door shut and collapsed in a heap on Kenny's bed, stuffing our hands in our mouths so that we wouldn't give ourselves away.

"Quick, Frankie, quick," said Rosie. "Get that off."

It's a good job she said that because we'd just ripped the gown off and collected up the finger nails which shot all over the floor, and stuffed them under Kenny's pillow, when Emma and Hayley crashed into the room.

"Molly says someone just broke into her room. Are you all OK? Did you hear anything? You'd better come and help us look." Then they raced out again.

We all looked at each other and tried to arrange our faces so they didn't give us away and followed them out onto the landing. Molly was still screaming her head off.

CHAPTER EIGHT

"It's all right, Molly," said Emma, trying to calm her down. "You can stop making that terrible noise. It sounds as if you're being murdered."

"I could have been," she yelled.

"Kenny, are you sure you didn't hear anything?" Emma asked again.

"Not a thing," said Kenny. "We were just fooling about in my room. We didn't hear a sound, except for Monster-face screaming her head off."

"So would you if someone had been

standing over your bed. Have you looked? He might still be in the house."

We offered to search the house. We all ran up and downstairs like mad things, opening doors then banging them closed again. We raced into the kitchen and it was a good job we did because the chicken masala was burning so we yelled up to tell them and Hayley rushed down to turn it off.

Emma was still trying to calm Molly down and get some sense out of her but Molly wouldn't stop yelling, "I want my mum! I want my dad!" She was really enjoying herself. She was putting on a good act, but I could tell she wasn't really scared. I didn't like the way she kept looking at us. Somehow I was sure she knew it was me.

"Look," said Emma, "just stop shouting. Mum and Dad'll be home any time. They'll sort it out." You could tell she didn't know what to do for the best.

"It'll be too late by then," Molly insisted. "He'll have got away. You've got to ring the police."

"Don't be stupid," said Kenny. "We can't ring the police. Anyway, we've looked. There's no one here. You probably dreamt it."

"I didn't dream it. He was right here, standing over me. He was six feet tall and he had horrible claws. He'd probably have clawed my eyes out if I hadn't woken up."

"She just dreamt it," Kenny told Emma. "Or made it up. She's always making things up. You know what she's like."

Emma certainly knew what Molly was like, but she could see something funny was going on. And any minute now we could all see Kenny and Molly were going to get into one of their screaming matches, so Emma said, "Kenny go away and leave this to me. Take the others back to your bedroom. Now!"

"But she's just being stupid and making

it all up," Kenny started again.

"I am not," Molly screamed.

"Go! Now!" said Emma pointing to the door.

Kenny gave Molly a last nasty look and then we all trooped back to her bedroom. We didn't close the door because we wanted to try and hear what was going on. But Emma closed hers so, however much we strained our ears, we couldn't hear a sound.

We sat on Kenny's bedroom floor trying to enjoy our revenge.

"Did you see her face?" hissed Kenny.

"It was awesome," said Lyndz.

"She sounded like a banshee," said Rosie.

"He was six feet tall with horrible claws," I said, mimicking Molly's voice.

We were all giggling and hugging ourselves, but we couldn't really keep it up for long, because we couldn't help wondering what Molly was telling Emma.

"What do you think's going on?" said Fliss. She looked really scared. I couldn't see why because I was the one who was going to get into trouble if anybody did.

"Oh, don't worry about it," said Kenny. "Emma'll calm her down. She won't want mum to know there's been trouble or she won't get paid for looking after us."

Oh well, we thought, if Kenny isn't worried, there's no reason for the rest of us to be. But a couple of minutes later we had plenty to be worried about.

Emma came in and said she'd phoned the police and they were sending someone round straight away. I thought Kenny was going into orbit.

"What! Why! What do you mean? Police? You didn't need to ring the police."

"Well," said Emma, "Molly says there was definitely someone in her room so there must have been a prowler or something. Anyway, don't you worry, the police'll sort it out. They should be round any minute."

Kenny almost grabbed hold of Emma. "Mum and Dad'll go mad you know. You should have waited for them to come back. You know what Molly's like; she makes things up all the time. They'll be so mad when they find out."

But Emma stayed dead cool. "No, I'm sure they'd have done the same. Anyway you needn't worry about it," she said as she left the room. "Although," she turned and added, "they'll probably want a statement from each of you."

"A statement?" shrieked Fliss. "But I didn't see anything. It was nothing to do with me. It wasn't my idea. I didn't do anything."

That's just like Fliss when she gets in a flap. I could have murdered her. Kenny looked as if she could too.

"Nobody suggested *you'd* done anything, Fliss," said Emma, looking straight at me. "If you didn't hear a sound that's what you'll need to say to the inspector."

"Inspector!" said Kenny.

"Well, whoever they send," said Emma smiling. "I'm going to get on with my meal until they come."

After she went out we all sat there too shocked to speak. We were all white, in fact we looked like a gang of ghosts. Now we were in deep trouble.

"You're going to have to go and tell them the truth," said Fliss.

"No way," said Kenny.

"I think Molly knows anyway," I said. The others looked at me. "I've just got this feeling. I think she could tell it was me."

"What? So you mean she's putting it all on just to get us into trouble."

I nodded. "I think so."

"I still think you'd better tell Emma," said Fliss. "So she can ring the police and tell them not to come."

Lyndz nodded. "I agree with Fliss. Your

mum and dad'll go mad if they come home and find the police here."

"They're going to go mad anyway," said Kenny. "Emma's bound to tell them and I'll be grounded for the rest of my life, or longer. And just coming up for Christmas as well. I'll probably get no presents, no Christmas dinner, no TV for the whole week." We were all feeling sorry for Kenny, but we were feeling sorry for ourselves too.

"Oh, please, Kenny, go and tell Emma," Fliss begged her. "Before they come."

I couldn't decide what was best. I sort of agreed with Fliss. Better make a clean breast of it before her parents came back. And yet I knew how much Kenny would hate having to own up and let Molly think she'd won. But time was running out. They could be here any moment. We were just waiting for the doorbell to ring. Kenny sat there and wouldn't speak. She looked as if she'd turned to stone or something.

"I think we should vote on it," said Fliss. "Who thinks Kenny should go and tell Emma the truth?" She put her own hand straight up. Lyndz hesitated, then shrugged her shoulders and put her hand up too. Rosie slowly lifted hers. Kenny looked at each of them as if they were no friends of hers. Then she looked at me. My hand felt like a lump of lead.

Kenny was my best friend. We'd been friends since playschool. I didn't want to let her down but I could feel my hand starting to rise. Suddenly we heard a car coming along the road, slowing down and turning into their drive.

We all just about had heart attacks. Kenny jumped up off the bed, raced downstairs and burst into the kitchen. We were all just a step behind her.

"OK, it was us. We did it. It was just a joke. We didn't mean to scare her to death. It was..." Kenny stopped in mid sentence.

Emma and Hayley and Molly were sitting

at the breakfast bar eating chicken masala. They were all grinning like three fat cats that had got the cream. There was a heavenly smell of bananas cooking and I just kept thinking how we wouldn't get any now.

The truth dawned on Kenny and her face screwed up. She was just about to start screaming at them, when the front door opened and in walked her mum and dad.

"Are you girls still up and about?" said Kenny's mum. "I thought you'd have been in bed by now. Off you go and get ready and I'll bring you all a drink up." Then she spotted Molly. "Well, you're looking a bit brighter. I told you all you needed was a good rest."

"Mmm, mmm," said Kenny's dad. "Something smells good. Any left over?"

"You be careful," said her mum. "You've just had that tooth fixed. We don't want any more accidents. I'll make you some scrambled egg."

"Oh, thanks a lot. Baby food. Just what I need."

We all headed off upstairs thinking, well, at least we'd got away without being interviewed by the police, when we heard Monster-face say, "By the way, Dad. I found the rest of that cake in the bin. I think I know what you broke your tooth on."

We didn't hang around to hear any more. We went straight off to bed.

CHAPTER NINE

We all got into our sleeping bags, apart from Fliss and Kenny who had the beds. We turned on our torches and lay there whispering.

"What do you think they'll say in the morning?" I asked Kenny.

"Dunno." She sounded as if she didn't care much either. She was so mad with Molly, that was all she could think about.

It was bad enough that Molly had told Emma it was us and then got Emma to pretend she'd rung the police, and we'd fallen for it. But now she'd grassed on us to Kenny's dad about the spider in the cake. That was really the pits.

"It's just not fair," said Kenny. "How is it she always wins?"

"She doesn't always win," I said. "She might have realised afterwards that it was me, but when she first woke up she was really scared. You should have seen her face. She looked as if she was going to wet herself."

"Yeah," said Lyndz. "It was worth it. What does it matter if we get grounded again. They always tell us we're grounded forever, but they soon forget."

That's true, isn't it? Grown-ups haven't got very long memories.

"And it's been the best sleepover yet," said Rosie. "I'll never forget this one."

"Really?" said Kenny.

"Coo-el," I agreed.

"Anyway it's not over yet," said Fliss. "We've still got our midnight feast to have and our Christmas presents."

"Yeah, but that's another thing," said Kenny, miserably. "I still haven't got any of your presents. I hadn't got enough money and now I won't be able to get any more." She sounded as if she might start to cry, which I'd never seen Kenny do before.

"Look, it doesn't matter," said Lyndz. "I've only got little presents this year. I couldn't afford anything big like Fliss."

"Nor me," said Rosie. "I don't have much money."

Fliss looked a bit embarrassed. "Well, I didn't really have to pay for the tapes," she admitted. "Andy got them cheap from the man who owns the shop. He did some plastering for him. Anyway," she said, "it's like my mum says, it's not the gift that counts…"

We all joined in, "It's the thought behind it."

So I felt a lot better after that. We agreed that Kenny and I would give the others their presents on the last day at school. Rosie gave us each a cute pencil with the head of Pongo from *101 Dalmations* on it and a matching rubber.

But Lyndz's present was the best surprise. It was one big flat box wrapped in Christmas paper with a label which said: *To the Sleepover Club*.

We didn't know what to make of it.

"But who's going to open it?" said Fliss.

"All of us," said Lyndz. "I'll count. One... two... three..."

We all tore a bit of the paper until it was unwrapped. Inside was a box of five Christmas crackers. We could see through the cellophane there was one with each of our names on it. They looked dead good, really professional, but Lyndz and her mum had made them themselves.

Before we pulled them we sat round in a circle and instead of our usual Sleepover Club song, we sang, "Happy Christmas to us, Happy Christmas to us, Happy

Christmas, to the Sleepover Club, Happy Christmas to us." When we pulled the crackers they went off with a bang, like proper ones and they had a party hat inside and a joke and a present and a chocolate. I got a key ring with a little black cocker spaniel on it, just like my dog, Pepsi. It was brilliant.

We sat up wearing paper hats, reading out our jokes and eating our chocolates. Then we sang loads of Christmas carols. After that we had our midnight feast and it really was midnight; we heard the church clock chiming twelve.

When we snuggled down into our sleeping bags and turned off our torches, Kenny said, "I don't care what they say tomorrow, it was a good laugh, so it was worth it."

"It sure was," I said. "The best." And everyone agreed.

GOODBYE

Kenny's mum and dad had had plenty of time to calm down by the time we went home, so Kenny didn't really get into mega-trouble. She did get a good telling off about putting things in cakes, though, because it could have been dangerous. As her dad pointed out, someone could have choked on it which, to be honest, we hadn't really thought about.

Kenny wouldn't speak to Emma at first for taking Molly's side, even though Emma insisted she hadn't. She said she thought that after what we'd done to Molly we deserved a bit of a scare ourselves.

Molly was dead pleased with herself, and kept rubbing it in, so Kenny refused to speak to her for a whole week. But she couldn't keep it up because then it was Christmas and Molly did such a surprising thing. She got Kenny her very best Christmas present ever. It was an amazing pop-up book all about the body, with pictures of your insides and bits that move, with all the really gory bits. Kenny loved it. Molly had been saving for weeks and in the end she'd had to borrow a bit from their mum. So, you see, even gruesome older sisters can surprise you sometimes.

They had a truce which lasted for most of Christmas. It's over now, of course, because Molly trod on Kenny's picture of Emile Heskey and wouldn't apologise. He's a footballer who plays for Leicester City and Kenny worships him. But now he's got a big footprint right across his nose. So it's back to normal bedroom warfare at Kenny's.

But there you go. It was still a pretty good Christmas. My mum was dead pleased with her pig and I had a brain wave which meant I didn't need to spend lots of money on my friends. I remembered the photo Dad took of us the last time they sleptover at my house when we had the wedding! So I had copies made and put them in little plastic frames and everyone was really pleased because we all looked drop-dead gorgeous.

Which reminds me – everyone *lurved* my new shoes. They are really drastic. I'm trying to persuade Mum and Dad to let me wear them for school. They've said, "No way. Not a chance. Don't even ask." But they always say that at first. It might take a while, but don't worry, I'll get round them.

Anyway keep your fingers crossed for me. See you some time. Bye.

Starring the Sleepover Club

CHAPTER ONE

Oh, hi! It's you again. Look, you can walk with me if you want to. I'm going to the video shop to borrow a film. But you've got to promise me one thing. You've got to promise that you won't ask me what happened at our sleepover last night. I can't tell you because it's a Big Secret. The Biggest. So don't ask me, OK?

My mum and dad said I could choose a film for the three of us to watch tonight. Usually one of them comes to the video shop with me and makes a big song and dance about which films are suitable, and which films aren't. You know what parents are like.

But today they said I could come on my own. I think it's because they're pretty relieved that nothing happened at the sleepover last night (or so they think). The last time we slept over at Fliss's, we ended up wrecking her mum's kitchen, as well as giving her gruesome neighbours a complete fit. This time we did something just as bad. We – oh, sorry! I forgot. I can't tell you.

Come on, here's the video shop. No, don't bother going into the adult section. I'm not even allowed to look at the covers of the films over there. Anyway, Nathan Wignall's standing there, trying to pretend he's old enough to borrow a grown-up film. I've told you about Nathan Wignall before, haven't I? He lives next door to me, and he's a complete pain. I could tell you loads of embarrassing stuff about Nathan Wignall, but I haven't got time right now.

We sometimes watch a video when we have a sleepover, but not every time. Like last night at Fliss's, we – whoops, there I go again! Me and my big mouth.

No, I can't tell you. Don't ask me to. My lips are sealed.

8

Look, don't get mad. Of *course* I trust you. As my grandma always says, if you can't trust your friends, who can you trust? It's just that if our parents find out what really went on at Fliss's house last night, we'll be up to our eyes in everlasting doom for the next five years. So, if I tell you what happened at the sleepover last night, do you swear never to breathe a WORD about it to ANYONE? Cross your heart and hope to die? Do you promise faithfully you won't tell anyone, even if they offer you their last Rolo?

OK, you've twisted my arm. I give in. Let's go behind the children's videos so that no one else can hear us, and I'll tell you all about it.

The sleepover at Fliss's was going to be an ordinary sleepover right up until the day before. Well, what I mean is, no sleepover is ever really ordinary, but we weren't expecting anything special to happen. Of course, we were wrong.

As my grandma always says, the best place to start is at the beginning. That was at school on Thursday morning. We were in the playground, and all of the Sleepover Club were there, except Fliss. Me (I'm Frankie, remember?), Kenny, Rosie and Lyndz. We were discussing our new teacher, Miss Jenkins. Our real teacher, Mrs Weaver, was ill and she hadn't been at school all week. We missed her a bit. But not a lot. Compared to Mrs Weaver, Miss Jenkins was a pushover.

"OK, today I'm going for it," Kenny said. "I bet I can make six trips to the pencil sharpener before Miss Jenkins tells me off."

"What's the record so far?" I asked.

"I managed five times yesterday," said Rosie.

Kenny shrugged. "You only got the fifth one because Danny McCloud had stuffed two rubbers up his nose. You sneaked over to the sharpener while Miss Jenkins was telling him off."

"Then they got stuck up there," said Lyndz. "Poor old Miss Jenkins had a terrible time trying to pull them out."

"I'm glad I'm not a teacher," I said with feeling. "I wouldn't put my fingers up Danny McCloud's nose for a billion pounds."

"Well, she couldn't just let Danny

suffocate, could she?" said Lyndz.

There was a thoughtful silence.

"I wouldn't have a problem with that," Kenny said with a perfectly straight face, and Rosie and I began to giggle.

"I think you're horrible," said Lyndz. "Poor Miss Jenkins. I feel—"

"Really sorry for her!" we all chimed in. Lyndz has got a heart of pure marshmallow.

"Oh, shut up!" Lyndz grinned, and stuck her tongue out at us. She's used to us winding her up. "By the way, where's Fliss?"

"Yeah, where *is* Fliss?" said Kenny. "She's going to be late if she doesn't get here soon."

We all looked at each other. Fliss is never late for school. She's the sort of person who's never late for anything, not even the dentist.

"Look, there she is." Rosie pointed across the playground. "What's the matter with her?"

Fliss was racing madly across the playground towards us, waving her arms in the air. Her face was bright red, and she was puffing and panting like she'd just run the London Marathon. She was so out of breath

11

that, when she skidded to a halt in front of us, she couldn't speak.

"What is it, Fliss?" I asked, feeling a bit alarmed.

Fliss took a huge breath.

"My mum and Andy have bought a camcorder, and my mum says we can video the sleepover tomorrow night!" she squealed.

"Really?" Rosie gasped, her eyes as round as dinner plates.

"Coo-el!" shrieked Kenny and Lyndz.

"You lucky thing, Fliss!" I said. I was green with jealousy. I'd been nagging my mum and dad for months to buy a camcorder. I'd tried everything from bribery (promising to do the dishes for a year), to tugging at the parental heartstrings (asking them how they'd feel when they had no videos of their little girl to watch when I'd grown up). My dad had said, "Relieved". I think he was joking.

"This is so cool," Kenny said happily. "We're going to have an official Sleepover Club video!"

"I'm going to ask my mum if I can get some

new pyjamas," Lyndz babbled excitedly.

"Me too," I said. My favourite Snoopy pyjamas were a bit too old and uninteresting to be on a video. Come to think of it, my sleeping bag was a bit old and uninteresting as well. I could do with a new one. That meant I was going to have to do some major sweet-talking to my mum and dad when I got home tonight.

Fliss was looking as smug as a cat who's eaten twenty cartons of cream. "That's not all," she said. "Andy says he'll make some copies of the video so that everyone can have their own."

That knocked us all out. We couldn't believe it.

"Fliss, you're the best," Kenny said enthusiastically.

Fliss beamed.

"We'll be able to watch our videos and remember what it was like to be in the Sleepover Club, when we're all old and wrinkly," she said.

"We can still carry on having sleepovers when we get old, though, can't we?" Lyndz asked anxiously.

13

"Course we can," I said. "But just in case we get too old and creaky to play International Gladiators—"

"Or in case we get too old and tired to stay up for midnight feasts," said Kenny.

"Or if we haven't got any teeth left to eat the midnight feasts," Rosie said.

"—we'll always have the videos to remind us," Fliss finished off.

"Oh, I can't wait for tomorrow night," Lyndz sighed. "It's going to be excellent."

We didn't know it then, but we wouldn't need a video to remind us of that sleepover at Fliss's. It was going to be a long, long time before any of us forgot it.

CHAPTER TWO

As I said before, I was really set on having new pyjamas for the Sleepover Event of the Century, so I started my campaign as soon as I got home that night.

"Mum," I said casually, "have you seen my Snoopy pyjamas recently?"

"Is that a trick question?" My mum was putting a family-size packet of vegetarian lasagne in the microwave. No-one cooks in our house, except for my dad's famous pizzas. We're a strictly "heat 'n' eat" family. "I saw them yesterday when I took them out of the washing-machine."

"No, I mean have you seen the state of

15

them." I pulled my Snoopy pyjamas from behind my back like a magician producing a white rabbit, and flapped them at my mum. "Look at them, they're gross."

My mum raised her eyebrows.

"I can't see anything wrong with them."

"Look!" I showed her the pyjama bottoms. One of the legs had started fraying after a sleepover at Rosie's when Kenny had grabbed me by the ankles and tried to throw me off the bed. I'd kind of helped it along a bit with my nail scissors. "I can't wear these at Fliss's sleepover tomorrow."

"Oh, Frankie, they're perfectly all right."

"No, they aren't," I persisted. Nagging is the only way to wear parents down. They'll do anything for a bit of peace and quiet. "I told you before, Fliss's mum is going to video the sleepover, and I need to look good."

"Frankie," my mum said, "this is a home video, not a Hollywood movie."

"I know. But these pyjamas are dangerous. What if they keep on unravelling while I'm asleep, and they unravel right up to my neck and strangle me?"

My mum looked at me over the top of her glasses.

"Have you been reading those 'Bonechillers' again?"

"Mum," I said solemnly, "I'm being straight with you here. I cannot wear these pyjamas to Fliss's sleepover tomorrow night."

"Fine." My mum opened the fridge and took out a packet of ready-washed salad. "It's lucky you have at least eight other pairs of pyjamas in your cupboard to choose from, then, isn't it?"

"Oh, Mum," I groaned. "Those aren't sleepover pyjamas. And anyway, they're all too small for me."

My mum shrugged. "That's life, Frankie."

Parents. They're so unreasonable. But I wasn't finished yet. I went out of the kitchen, and into the living-room where my dad was laying the table and watching the news on the telly at the same time.

"Guess what, Dad?" I gave him my Best-Behaved Daughter of the Year smile. "Fliss's mum's bought a camcorder, and she's going to video our sleepover tomorrow."

"Really," my dad said absently, his eyes

17

fixed on the TV.

"So I was hoping I could get a new pair of pyjamas. Could you pick me up after school tomorrow and drive me into Leicester?"

"Sure, sweetheart."

Like taking sweets from a baby.

"Thanks, Dad!" I said, just as my mum came in with the plates.

"Thanks for what?" she asked suspiciously.

"Er – yes, thanks for what?" The news had finished now, and my dad was looking bewildered.

"Dad says he'll drive me into town after school tomorrow to buy some new pyjamas for the sleepover," I said.

My mum put the plates down on the table with a thump.

"Francesca Theresa Thomas, you are the most cunning and devious child I've ever met."

"That's what comes of having lawyers for parents," I said. "By the way, my sleeping bag's looking a bit gross too."

"Don't push your luck, Frankie," said my dad.

"OK, OK. But I really do need new jim-jams.

I want to look good in our video."

"So," said my dad, "we're finally going to see what goes on at these famous sleepovers, are we?"

"I already know what goes on," my mum said, dishing up the lasagne. "Chaos, trouble and lots of junk food."

"There's a bit more to it than that," I said, picking up my fork. "And anyway, we aren't going to let just anyone watch the video. Sleepovers are supposed to be a secret."

Especially from parents. I wasn't quite sure how we were going to get away with keeping what we did at our sleepovers a secret if Fliss's mum was going to be filming us. But I'd worry about that later.

First of all, though, we had to get through Friday at school. It was pretty difficult because we were all hyper-excited about the sleepover that night, and by the end of the day, we'd turned Miss Jenkins into a nervous wreck. Kenny had managed a record eleven trips to the pencil sharpener without being spotted, and we'd played Pass the Sniff in silent reading until our noses hurt.

As soon as the home bell rang, the Sleepover Club were first out of the classroom door.

"My dad's taking me shopping," I told the others. "I'm going to get some new pyjamas for tonight."

"I've already got some," said Kenny. "They're so cool. They're going to be the coolest pyjamas ever seen on video.'"

"What are they like?" asked Lyndz, but Kenny shook her head.

"You'll have to wait and see!"

"Oh, I can't wait for tonight!" Fliss squealed, and we all grinned. Tonight was going to be really special.

I got a wicked pair of pyjamas in Leicester. They were bright orange – I mean really bright, the colour of an ice lolly – and they had apples and bananas printed all over them. There was a matching pair of fluffy orange slippers too, although I had to promise to wash up the dinner plates for two weeks to get my hands on those. By the time we got back home, I had an hour to get ready for the sleepover.

First I packed my sleepover kit. In went my

new pyjamas and slippers, my diary, my toothbrush, my teddy bear, Stanley, a big bag of fun-size Mars bars, a family-size pack of cheese and onion crisps, my torch and personal stuff like a hairbrush and deodorant. Next I had to decide what I was going to wear. Usually we just wear jeans and tee-shirts, so that we can slob out and do exactly what we like, but tonight was different. Tonight I was going to wear my black hipster flares and my new lime-green shirt. And I was going to crimp my hair.

I don't crimp my hair very often, because it takes ages, but I really wanted to look good in our sleepover video. After I'd done my hair, I painted my nails silver. I love silver nail varnish, and I'm allowed to wear it sometimes at weekends, if The Oldies are in a good mood. I was hoping that tonight I could get away without them noticing.

Wait a minute, the man at the video shop desk is giving us funny looks. Maybe we ought to pretend we're looking at the films. Come on, Nathan's over the other side of the shop now, so we should be OK. Just keep an eye out for him, that's all.

Well, when I finally made it downstairs, carrying my sleepover kit and my sleeping bag, my dad raised his eyebrows.

"What happened to that scruffy little girl who used to be our daughter?" he said to my mum.

"Oh, zip it, Dad," I said. "I just threw on the first things I could find."

"It looks like you just threw on some silver nail varnish too," said my mum.

"This is a special occasion, Mum," I said. "When I'm a famous actress, people will be paying thousands of pounds to get their hands on this video."

Did I mention to you that I want to be an actress when I grow up? That's why I was really looking forward to tonight. It was going to be my very first chance to see myself on film.

"Come on then, Michelle Pfeiffer," said my mum, "I'll run you over to Fliss's."

"OK," I said. Fliss doesn't live that far away from us, but I had all my sleepover stuff to carry, and besides, it looked like it was going to rain, which would wash all the crimping out of my hair quicker than you can say "Bad Hair Day".

"Mum," I said when we were in the car and on our way, "can we—?"

"No," said my mum.

"What do you mean, no?" I glared at her. "You didn't even know what I was going to say."

"Oh, yes I do." My mum turned into Fliss's road. "You were going to say, 'Can we get a camcorder?'"

I was speechless. Parents can really make you mad sometimes, can't they?

"Well, why can't we?"

"Because they're too expensive, that's why," my mum said. "Do you know how much they cost, Frankie? Six or seven hundred pounds. Which reminds me." We stopped at some traffic lights, and she turned to look hard at me. "No fooling around tonight. Do exactly what Fliss's mum tells you. Because if anything happens to that camcorder, you and your friends are going to be paying for it out of your pocket money for a very, very long time."

"Oh, Mum," I groaned as we pulled up outside Fliss's house. "Have I ever let you down before?"

"Yes, you have."

"Bye, then," I said quickly, and dived out of the car before she could get launched on a list of sleepover disasters.

I was just about to open Fliss's gate when Kenny's dad's car pulled up, and Kenny jumped out. I stared at her. She was still wearing her Leicester City top because that's all she ever wore when she wasn't at school. But she wasn't wearing her favourite pair of jeans with holes in the knees or her Timberland boots. Instead she was wearing brand-new jeans and proper shoes. With heels. And she'd only gone and crimped her hair.

"You've crimped your hair!" I said.

"So have you!" Kenny stared back at me, and we both started to laugh. "We're going to look like twins on this video!"

A little red car stopped by the kerb while we were still laughing. Rosie's mum waved to us from the driver's seat, and then Rosie got out. She looked really cool in a long skirt and

24

a matching top. And her hair was crimped.

Rosie looked at me and Kenny, and her face went pink.

"You've crimped your hair!" she gasped.

"I think we've already had this conversation," said Kenny.

"We're triplets now!" I said, and we all started to giggle.

Then I looked over Kenny's shoulder, and saw Lyndz walking up the road with her brother Tom. Lyndz looked good in a pink skirt and a black top. But guess what she'd done to her hair?

"Oh-oh," I said. "Crimped hair alert!"

"Oh!" Lyndz gasped when she saw the rest of us. "You've—"

"Crimped your hair!" we all chimed in. "Just like you!"

"Wow," Tom said, grinning all over his face. "Looks like a hairdresser's worst nightmare."

Lyndz gave him a shove.

"Get lost, moron," she said.

Still laughing, Tom went off, and we all stood outside Fliss's house, and looked at each other and our crimped hair.

"Oh, well," said Lyndz with a big grin, "I think we all look great."

"Come on," Kenny said, pushing open the gate. "I'm dying to get inside and get filmed!"

We all hurried up the path. I rang the bell, and Fliss opened the door. She was wearing a spotless, cream-coloured lacy dress with matching tights and shoes, and her hair was piled high on her head. It had been stuck with pins all over to keep it up, and it looked pretty uncomfortable. She took one look at our hair, and burst out laughing.

"You've all crimped your hair!"

"Yes, we had noticed," I said.

"Is that the girls, Fliss?" Andy, Fliss's mum's boyfriend, came out of the living-room with a camcorder balanced on his shoulder. He stopped and moved it slowly in our direction. Immediately we all started squealing and giggling and shoving each other.

"Come on, girls, give us a smile!" Andy said.

We all began to wave and smile at the camera. This was certainly going to be one sleepover we would never forget.

CHAPTER THREE

So there we all were, sitting in a row on Mrs Sidebotham's cream-coloured sofa, trying not to look bored out of our skulls. Which we were, actually.

"Oh, come on, girls." Andy sighed from behind the camcorder. "Do something interesting, can't you?"

We all looked down at our feet. Andy sighed again, and lowered the camcorder.

"What's the matter with you?" he said, "You don't usually sit here and do nothing when you come round for one of these sleepovers, do you?"

We all looked at each other. No, of course

we didn't usually sit there and do nothing when we had a sleepover. But today was different. Today we were being filmed, and although Andy wasn't exactly Fliss's real dad, he was still sort of like a parent. That meant that some of the things we might have done, we couldn't do. So the safest thing was to sit on the sofa and do absolutely nothing. After all, as my grandma says, why go looking for trouble?

When we'd first arrived at Fliss's, it had been fun being filmed. Fliss's mum had made a great big tea, and we'd all sat down to eat, while Andy kept dodging around the table trying to film us all. It took us about ten minutes to get over the urge to wave and grin like an idiot every time he pointed the camera in our direction, and then after that we were OK.

It was after tea was over that things started to go wrong. If it had been a normal sleepover, there were lots of things we could have done. Sometimes we just used to sit and talk, until it was time to go to bed. But a lot of the things we talked about were Private and Top Secret, and we didn't feel like talking about things like that with Andy and his camcorder sticking to us like glue.

One of the other things we do when we go to Fliss's is think of ways to annoy her snobby neighbours. They're called Charles and Jessica Watson-Wade (yes, really) and they have a baby called Bruno, which I thought was a dog's name. The last time we slept over at Fliss's, we had a killer of a time winding-up the Watson-Wades. Fliss's mum went mad (and so did every other mum and dad), but it was worth it. The problem was, how could we play Winding-up the Watson-Wades when Andy and his camera were right behind us?

So Kenny had suggested that we played barging contests, one of our International Gladiators games. One person's the horse, the other's the rider, and you have to barge the other horse and rider off the lawn in the back garden. We always play barging contests when we sleepover at Fliss's, because there's not much else we can do. Fliss's bedroom is too small for really tough stuff, and we can't do anything inside because her mum is so house-proud. But the garden's quite big, and we can play barging contests out there as much as we want to.

Not today, though. Fliss had gone pale at the very thought.

"I can't, not with my hair up like this," she'd said. "It'd drop down in one minute flat."

"I don't want to play either," Lyndz said. "I've got to keep my new clothes clean."

Rosie didn't say anything, but she didn't look too keen herself. That was probably because she was wearing a long skirt, and she'd have to hitch it up and tuck it into her knickers. I didn't say anything either. I didn't want to get my best ankle boots dirty. After all, it had taken me three months to persuade my parents to buy them.

Kenny had rolled her eyes, looking disgusted.

"What a bunch of wimps," she said, but we wouldn't give in. No barging contests. And that was why we were all sitting in a row of the sofa, bored out of our minds and twiddling our thumbs, which is definitely not what a sleepover is supposed to be about.

"Are you all having a good time, girls?"

Fliss's mum asked us brightly as she came into the living-room.

"Yes, thank you, Mrs Sidebotham," we all said dutifully, lying through our teeth.

"If you hear me snoring, pinch me," Kenny whispered in my ear. I bit my lip to stop myself from laughing, but Andy was still onto us like a shot.

"What did you say to Frankie, Kenny?" he asked eagerly. "Come on, say it again and I can video it."

Kenny shook her head.

"I can't," she said solemnly. "It was secret sleepover business."

"Oh." Andy looked really disappointed. "Well, you girls must want to do *something*?"

There was a note of desperation in his voice, which made me feel quite sorry for him.

"Why don't you play Monopoly?" suggested Fliss's mum.

"Oh, great big fat hairy deal," I heard Kenny mutter. It's not that we don't like Monopoly, we do. It was just that we thought our sleepover video would be a bit more radical than this.

31

Fliss went off to get the Monopoly box, but by this time Andy had had enough, and said he was off to the pub. So Fliss's mum took over the camera. She didn't film the whole game, which was lucky because it went on for hours. She filmed the beginning, then she stopped to watch *Brookside*, and then she filmed the end, when Rosie won. Rosie had Mayfair and Park Lane, and she cleaned the rest of us out.

"Right, time for you girls to go up to bed," Fliss's mum said when we'd finished the game. "I thought it might be nice if I filmed you going up the stairs, and waving goodnight. Then you can watch the video in the morning before you go home."

By this time I was sick of being filmed, and I think the others were too, but we couldn't very well say so, could we? So we trailed out into the hall, and followed each other up the stairs. Fliss's mum stood at the bottom, shouting instructions at us.

"Come on, girls, turn around and wave at me. Nice big smiles. No, Kenny, we don't want to see your tongue, thank you."

"Aren't you coming upstairs with us, Mrs

Sidebotham?" asked Lyndz. "You could film us putting on our new pyjamas."

Fliss's mum looked shocked. "Oh no, Lyndsey. I don't think that would be very nice at all."

"But you don't get to see anything," said Kenny. "We change inside our sleeping bags. It's a great laugh."

Fliss's mum shook her head firmly. "No, I don't think so. Now off you go. It's getting late."

We all trailed upstairs, and into Fliss's bedroom. I honestly couldn't remember a more boring sleepover. And to think we'd all been so excited... Even Fliss looked miserable.

No one said anything in front of Fliss, but when she'd gone to the bathroom, Kenny flopped onto one of the beds, and groaned.

"I hope no-one ever watches that video, or they'll think that sleepovers are some kind of punishment," she said.

"Tonight was the pits," I said. "I've had more fun at the dentist's."

"Don't say anything to Fliss," Lyndz said. "It wasn't her fault. We all wanted to be filmed too."

We all nodded, and trailed gloomily over to our bags to get our pyjamas. Sleepovers were supposed to be fun, and this one definitely wasn't. For just about the first time ever at a sleepover, I wished I was back at home in my bedroom, on my own. Oh well, I told myself, the best part of the sleepover hadn't happened yet.

I cheered up a bit when I opened my bag, and saw my brand-new orange pyjamas.

"Wow, they're really wild," said Lyndz, who was looking over my shoulder. "Look at mine." Lyndz's new jim-jams were yellow with big pink flowers all over them.

"They're not as cool as mine," said Kenny. She took her pyjamas out of her bag, and we all burst out laughing. They were black, with white skulls all over them.

"They're a killer, aren't they?" said Kenny. "I got them from a boy's shop. I had to nag my mum like crazy to get them. She said they'd give me nightmares."

Rosie grabbed her bag, and pulled out her own pyjamas, which had teddy-bears all over them.

"Bet you I'm changed first!" she yelled, diving into her sleeping bag. We all squealed, and leapt into our own sleeping-bags, pulling off our clothes as fast as we could. I joined in, although I always lose. I'm just too tall and my arms and legs are too long. I didn't mind not winning though, because it was a good laugh. And, boy, it was the first good laugh we'd had all evening.

Fliss came back from the bathroom just as we all finished changing. She still looked a bit miserable.

"Oh, come on, Fliss, cheer up," said Rosie. "I've brought toffee popcorn for the midnight feast, and you can have it all if you want."

Fliss loves toffee popcorn. Her face lit up.

"Thanks, Rosie," she said, but she didn't have time to say anything else because just then Lyndz hit Kenny right on the behind with a squishy-poo (that's a sleeping bag filled with clothes, in case you didn't know). Kenny went flying, and landed on one of the beds with her bottom in the air. We all screamed with laughter, and started belting each other with our own squishy-poos. This sleepover was getting better by the minute.

By the time Fliss's mum put her head round the door twenty minutes later, we were all tucked up. Fliss and Rosie were in the two beds, and Kenny, Lyndz and I were in our sleeping bags between them on the floor.

"Goodnight, girls," she said. "Sleep tight."

"Goodnight."

She closed the door. We lay there in the dark and counted up to twenty-five, then we switched our torches on.

"What shall we do first?" Fliss asked.

"Eat!" the rest of us said.

I don't know why we bother calling them midnight feasts, because we never make it to midnight. We always seem to be starving the moment we switch our torches on.

"This is the best bit of sleepovers," said Lyndz, handing round some chocolate biscuits.

"Yeah, this is the real sleepover, what's happening now. It's a pity we can't film it," said Kenny.

And of course, that's where the disaster really started...

CHAPTER FOUR

So there we were having our midnight feast, and Kenny had just said that it was a shame we couldn't film the stuff we did after lights out. Everybody agreed with her, but nobody really thought much about it at the time. Instead, we ate all the crisps and chocolates we'd brought (and Fliss ate most of Rosie's popcorn), and then we wrote in our diaries.

"What shall we do now?" Lyndz asked, when we'd finished writing.

"We could tell jokes," I suggested.

"No, let's have stories," said Kenny. "Horror stories."

"No," Fliss wailed. "They give me nightmares."

"I think we should do what Fliss wants," said Rosie. "After all, it's her sleepover."

"I want to practise our dance routine for next Friday," Fliss said firmly.

We're always working out dance routines. It's one of our best skives because we get to practise them in the school hall when all the other kids have been chucked out to play in the cold. Mrs Poole, our headteacher, lets us do the routines in Friday assembly, which is always a great laugh.

"Good idea," said Lyndz.

So we all got out of our beds and sleeping bags, and lined up in the space between the two beds. Fliss's bedroom isn't very big, so we had to stand on top of the sleeping bags. When we were all standing next to each other, there wasn't room to move our arms, never mind our legs, but we had a go. Then we got bored with trying to dance in such a tiny space, and instead we started pushing each other off the floor and onto the beds. Once you were bounced onto a bed, you were out. Eventually there was just me and Rosie left, and I really had to give her a mighty shove to get her off the floor. She bounced onto Fliss's bed, and landed right on top of Kenny.

"Oi!" Kenny spluttered. "Do you mind!" She picked up the nearest pillow, and hit out at her. Rosie ducked smartly, and the pillow thwacked Lyndz round the head instead. It was like something out of a silent movie.

By this time we were all laughing so hard, my sides really hurt.

"Sssh!" Fliss pleaded between giggles. "You'll wake my mum up!"

"Oh, that was excellent," I said, flopping down on the bed next to Kenny. "I wish I had a picture of Lyndz's face when Kenny hit her with that pillow!"

"We would have had a picture of it if we were filming with the camcorder," said Kenny.

"OK, OK," said Fliss impatiently. "But I don't know what you expect me to do about it."

I could see Kenny's eyes glinting wickedly in the light of my torch.

"Well, we could film ourselves…"

Fliss turned so white, she looked like a

ghost. So did Rosie. Even I was a bit taken aback, and I'm used to Kenny's mad ideas.

"What?" said Lyndz, who's sometimes a bit slow on the uptake. "How could we do that?"

"Simple," said Kenny. "Fliss borrows the camcorder, and then we can film ourselves doing real Sleepover Club things."

"NO," said Fliss.

"OK, OK, don't get in a razz," said Kenny. "If you don't know how to work the camcorder, just say so."

"It's not that," said Fliss quickly. She hates us to think that she can't do anything and everything. "Andy showed me how to use it when he wanted me to film him and mum doing the garden."

Kenny shrugged.

"So what's the problem then?"

Fliss opened her mouth, then closed it again. I guessed that what she'd been about to say was that she wasn't allowed to touch the camcorder unless her mum or Andy were around to supervise.

"Camcorders are really expensive," said Rosie. "I don't think Fliss's mum would be

40

too pleased if we used it without her permission."

Fliss shrugged. "I can do it, no problem," she said airily. "I'll fetch it now."

"Nice one, Fliss!" Kenny began applauding, and so did Lyndz. I was pleased too. After all, the official sleepover video had been about as interesting as watching paint dry so far. But I couldn't help hearing my mum's voice faintly in the back of my mind. "Remember if anything happens to that camcorder, you and your friends will be paying for it out of your pocket-money for years to come..."

I pushed the thought away.

"Come with me, Frankie," Fliss was saying nervously. "I don't want to go on my own."

"Where are we going?" I asked.

"To the spare bedroom. That's where my mum keeps the camcorder." Fliss picked up her torch, and gave the others a warning look. "The rest of you be quiet until we get back."

Fliss and I went out onto the dark landing. Fliss's mum and Andy were in bed, and so was her brother Callum. I have to say, it gave me a really funny feeling to be creeping about someone else's house in the dark in the middle of the night. I felt like a burglar.

"This is the spare room." Fliss stopped so suddenly that I bumped right into her. "We've got to be careful. The door squeaks like mad."

I reached for the handle and pushed the door open a little way. It gave a loud, frightening creak, the kind of noise you'd expect if you were entering a haunted house. My heart began to bump, and my hands felt clammy.

"Sssh!" Fliss whispered.

"I couldn't help it," I hissed back. I gave the door one more tiny shove, so that it was just open wide enough for us to squeeze in. It gave another ear-splitting creak, and we held our breath. But no-one came to see what was going on.

We slipped inside.

"Hold the torch while I get the camcorder out of the cupboard," Fliss said in my ear.

Curiously I played the torch around the room while Fliss was getting the camcorder. I'd never been in the spare bedroom before, and it didn't look anything like our spare bedroom at home. Our spare room is full of junk and bits and pieces like headless Sindy dolls, old newspapers and cookery books no-one uses. But Fliss's spare room was done up like a house in a magazine. There were flouncy blinds at the windows which matched the cover on the bed, and there were cupboards built all along one wall. There was also a headless person standing in the corner.

I couldn't help gasping, even though I clapped my hand over my mouth to muffle the sound. Fliss jumped a mile into the air, and nearly dropped the camcorder box.

"What's the matter with you?" she said under her breath.

"Did you know there's a headless person over there in the corner?" I said breathlessly.

"That's my mum's dress-making dummy, you idiot." Fliss pushed me towards the door. "Come on. If anyone wakes up, we're dead."

We hurried back to Fliss's bedroom. As soon as we got there, the others crowded round us as Fliss put the camcorder box carefully on the bed.

"Excellent!" said Kenny. "Come on, let's get started."

"Just a minute," said Lyndz. "Fliss's mum is going to know we borrowed the camcorder, isn't she?"

"What do you mean?" asked Kenny.

"Well, when we watch the video tomorrow morning, she's going to see all the bits we record now, when we're supposed to be asleep," said Lyndz.

We all looked at each other.

"Oh, rats," said Kenny. "What do we do now?"

"Easy," said Rosie. "We take the film out of the camcorder when we've finished, and put in a new blank tape. Then Andy and Fliss's mum will think it didn't record for some reason."

We all stared admiringly at Rosie. My mum says I'm devious, but I'm just a beginner compared to Rosie.

"Excellent idea," said Kenny. "Fliss, you have got a spare blank tape, haven't you?"

Fliss nodded.

"We've got loads."

"Great." Kenny gave a sigh of relief, and opened the camcorder box. "OK, let's get started!"

"We'll have to put the light on," I said. "Our torches won't be bright enough."

"What if someone sees the light under my door?" Fliss said nervously.

"Oh, you just put some clothes or a towel down to block it out," said Rosie. "I do it all the time when I want to read late. My mum never knows."

It was right at that very moment that we heard footsteps coming softly down the hall.

"Quick!" hissed Lyndz. "Someone's coming!"

For a second we were all frozen to the spot. Then we turned off our torches, and leapt for our beds and sleeping bags. Because Fliss's room is so small and we were so panicked, we kept bumping into each other in the dark before we managed to grope our way to our beds. It took me a few seconds to fold all my arms and legs in, and it was only when I was safely inside with my eyes tight shut that I remembered the box with the camcorder in it. But it was too late now.

Someone was opening the door...

CHAPTER FIVE

It was Fliss's mum. She put her head round the door and whispered, "Are you girls asleep?"

No one made a sound. I don't know about the others, but I was holding my breath so hard my lungs were bursting. Fliss's mum stood there looking into the room for what seemed like hours. Then she shut the door gently, and we could hear her footsteps going down the landing. We waited until we heard her bedroom door close. Then we all sat up, and Kenny crept across the room and flipped the light switch on.

"Wow, that was close," she said. "We only

just made it."

"I thought she'd see the camcorder on Rosie's bed, and we'd be done for," said Lyndz. "She must have heard Fliss and Frankie walking around."

Fliss was as white as a sheet.

"Thank goodness my mum didn't notice the camcorder!"

"By the way, where *is* the camcorder?" I said.

We all looked at Rosie's bed. We'd left the camcorder box sitting right there on the pink bedcover. But it wasn't there now.

"Don't panic," said Rosie calmly. She threw back her duvet cover, and there was the box nestling underneath. "I managed to grab it just before Mrs Sidebotham came in."

Fliss almost collapsed with relief.

"Thanks, Rosie," was all she could manage to say.

"Come on, then, are we going to make a video or what?" Impatiently Kenny grabbed the box, and began pulling the cardboard flaps open.

"Be careful!" Fliss hissed under her breath. "Let me do it!"

We all waited expectantly as Fliss unwrapped the camcorder from its box as carefully as if it was the Crown Jewels.

"We ought to decide what we're going to do," said Lyndz.

"Oh, don't be so boring," said Kenny. "Let's just mess around. What do you reckon, Rosie?"

"Yeah, that sounds cool," Rosie agreed. "As long as Fliss doesn't mind," she added quickly.

Fliss was too busy fiddling with the camcorder to hear.

"Right, I'm going to start recording," she announced, putting the machine up to her eye. "I'm starting now."

Kenny immediately leapt forward and stuck her face right up to the lens.

"Welcome to the Sleepover Club!" she said with a huge grin.

Fliss leapt backwards as if she'd been bitten.

"You nearly frightened me to death, Kenny!" she said, while the rest of us rolled around in fits of laughter. "Do it properly, or I'll put the camcorder away right now."

"OK, Mum," said Kenny. "How about this then?"

She grabbed a hairbrush from Fliss's dressing-table, and spoke into it as if it was a microphone.

"We'd like to welcome you all to this very special meeting of the Sleepover Club. My name is Kenny, and if you ever call me Laura MacKenzie, I'll thump you."

"Don't make me laugh," Fliss said between giggles, "or the camera will shake too much."

"Let me introduce you to the other members," Kenny said into her hairbrush. "This is Lyndsey Collins, known as Lyndz." Kenny pointed at Lyndz, who was sitting on Fliss's bed. "She's the nicest person I know, and she's always got the hiccups."

"Oh, don't, Kenny!" Lyndz said in between giggles, as Fliss turned the camera on her. "Don't start me off!"

"Well, you ought to be hiccuping," said Kenny. "It won't be a proper sleepover if you don't. Come on, can't you manage just one little hiccup for the camera?"

Just for once, Lyndz couldn't. She was

laughing so hard she had to hide her head under Fliss's pillow.

"Over here, Fliss." Kenny pointed at me. "Frankie next. Come on, Fliss, do I have to be the director as well as the star?"

"Give me a chance," Fliss moaned, turning the camera slowly in my direction.

"This is Frankie, my best mate," said Kenny. "No, you're not seeing things. She really is as tall as a house. We reckon her parents water her with liquid manure every night."

"Shut up, lamebrain," I said, and chucked a pillow at her.

"And this is Rosie..." Kenny waited for Fliss to turn slowly in her direction. "Rosie's got loads of good ideas for fooling parents. She's really cool." Kenny chucked the hairbrush onto the bed, "OK, that's everyone."

"What about me?" Fliss wailed from behind the camera.

"Oh, yeah, sorry, I forgot about you. Here," Kenny held out her hand, "give me the camera and I can film you. Then we'll all be in it."

"No way," said Fliss. "No one's doing any videotaping except me."

Kenny shrugged. "Please yourself." She picked up her hairbrush again. "Sorry, I missed out Fliss. Fliss is the Queen of the Sleepover Club, because this is her sleepover and her camcorder, and she's letting us use it, which is really excellent."

Fliss grinned.

"That's better," she said. "Now stop hogging the camera, Kenny. Let someone else have a go."

"It's a shame we've eaten our midnight feast," said Lyndz. "We could have filmed ourselves stuffing our faces."

"Never mind, you can talk about it instead," said Kenny, and she pushed the hairbrush into Lyndz's hand.

Lyndz began to giggle as Fliss turned the camera on her.

"Um – OK, midnight feasts. We always, always have a midnight feast when we sleepover—"

"More like a ten-thirty feast," I butted in.

"Sssh!" Kenny slung one of Fliss's cuddly toys at me. "Lyndz is talking."

Lyndz wasn't, actually. She was still giggling.

"Stop it, Lyndz!" said Fliss. "Say something interesting."

So Lyndz did. She gave a huge hiccup. We all burst out laughing, and had to bury our heads in our pillows to muffle the sound.

"Don't just – hic! – sit there – hic! – laughing!" said Lyndz. "Someone – hic! – help me!"

We've tried all the usual ways of getting Lyndz's hiccups to stop, but the best way is for someone to press down hard with their thumbs on the palm of her hand while she holds her breath. Don't ask me why this works. It just does.

The others were laughing too hard to be of any use, so I grabbed Lyndz's hand, and pressed down hard. Lyndz held her breath for so long, she started to turn crimson, but when she finally breathed out, her hiccups were gone.

"Thanks, Frankie," she said, gulping in a huge lungful of air.

"Come on," said Fliss impatiently. "I'm wasting loads of tape when you're not doing anything interesting."

"What about our sleepover song?" said Lyndz.

"Yes, let's sing it," said Rosie.

"But we don't sing that till we're about to go to sleep," Kenny groaned.

"We don't have to go to sleep," Lyndz argued. "We can just sing it so Fliss can video us."

"Go on then," said Fliss. "Don't bother with the actions, just do the song."

When we do our sleepover song, we're usually all tucked up in our sleeping bags with our torches on. When we get to the end of the song, the first one of us to lie down flat turns her torch off, and then we carry on till everyone's out.

"You three do the song," said Kenny. "I'm going to have a rest. I'm tired out." She put her hand up to her head and said in a fake American accent, "Being a star is so exhausting."

"Get her," I scoffed. "Come on, let's do the song then."

So we started singing:

"Down by the river there's a hanky-panky

53

With a bullfrog sitting on the hanky-panky—"

I could just see Kenny looking in her sleepover bag out of the corner of my eye.

"—With an Ooh Aah, Ooh Aah,
Hey, Mrs Zippy, with a One-Two-Three – OUT!"

Just before we got to "OUT!", which is when we try to be first to lie down if we're doing the actions, Kenny popped up behind us. When we sang "OUT!", she belted Rosie with her teddy bear.

"Ow!" Rosie jumped onto her bed. "I'll get you for that, Kenny!" She grabbed her own teddy bear, and waved it round her head. "Come on then, if you think you're hard enough!"

"Ooh, you don't frighten me!" Kenny scoffed. She jumped onto Rosie's bed, and next minute they were battling away whacking each other with their teddies, trying to knock each other's bear out of their hand. I love teddy fights, because my bear Stanley, who's as tough as old boots, always wins. Stanley was sitting on my pillow looking really left out, so I grabbed him and shoved him under Lyndz's nose.

"Stanley's challenging your bear to a fight to the death," I said.

Lyndz groaned. "Do I have to? We always lose."

"Come on, Lyndz!" I jumped onto Fliss's bed. "You don't want your teddy to be known as the wimp of Teddyland, do you?"

Lyndz grabbed her teddy, and climbed up onto Fliss's bed. We started jumping up and down and whacking each other, while Fliss videoed us.

"Be quiet – please!" Fliss kept pleading from behind the camera, but it's hard to be really quiet when you're playing teddy fights. Anyway, we all know that we can be fairly noisy when we sleep over at Fliss's, because her mum's bedroom is right at the other end of a very long landing. In fact, we know exactly how much noise we can make before Mrs Sidebotham comes charging in to tell us off.

Kenny and Rosie were still fighting it out on the other bed, and Lyndz and I were battling away too. At first I let Lyndz get a few whacks at Stanley in, so she didn't get too downhearted, but then I went in for the kill. Stanley headbutted her bear so hard that Lyndz went flying. She managed to stop herself on the edge of the bed, but she was wobbling so much she couldn't get her balance. She wobbled and she teetered and she wobbled, and for a second or two she looked as if she was going to make it. It was touch and go, and it was so funny that even Kenny and Rosie stopped bashing each other's bears to watch. But in the end the force of gravity was just too much for Lyndz. She went head-over-heels, and landed flat on the floor. Luckily the sleeping bags were piled up in a heap, so she didn't hurt herself, or make too much noise.

"That was brilliant, Lyndz!" I laughed. "Just like a stuntwoman!"

"I loved the way you just wobbled around on the edge of the bed for about five minutes!" said Kenny. "It was so cool."

Lyndz sat up, rubbing her behind.

"Thank goodness the sleeping bags were there, or I might have broken my leg!"

Rosie was looking thoughtful.

"Hey, you know what?" she said, and she sounded really excited. "I've just had a brilliant idea."

And that was when things really started to go downhill…

CHAPTER SIX

Come on, let's choose a film, and I'll tell you the rest of the story on the way home. How about *Mrs Doubtfire*? I've seen it before, but I don't mind seeing it again. I'll just take it up to the counter, and get it checked out.

Right, let's go – and make sure Nathan Wignall isn't following us. I wouldn't put anything past that little creep.

OK, we're in the clear. And remember, you've got to promise not to tell anyone what I'm going to tell you now...

Well, Rosie had this brilliant idea which turned out to be totally non-brilliant, but we all loved it at the time.

"Look," she said, "Why don't we send that video of Lyndz to *You've Been Framed*?"

"What a totally cool idea!" Kenny said immediately. "The Sleepover Club on TV – excellent!"

"We could make loads of money too," Rosie said breathlessly. "They pay for the best videos."

"How much?" Lyndz asked, her eyes wide.

"About two hundred pounds," Rosie said. "Or it might be more."

"Two hundred quid!" Kenny gasped. "I'm in!"

"Before you start counting the money," I said, "there's just one thing you've forgotten. If we end up splashed all over the TV, our parents are going to find out we borrowed the camcorder without Mrs Sidebotham's permission."

We all looked at each other. Then Kenny shrugged. "So what? They'll probably be so proud to see us on TV, they won't care."

"Or we can try to make sure our parents don't see the programme," Rosie chimed in.

"We can talk our way out of it somehow,"

Kenny added. "Come on, Frankie, don't be so boring."

"Oh, all right," I said. I didn't need much persuading. I was dying to be on TV. It was one of my biggest ambitions.

"What about you, Lyndz?" Kenny said. "You're the star, after all."

Lyndz giggled.

"Let's go for it," she agreed, "What do you think, Fliss?"

It was then that we realised that Fliss hadn't said anything for the last five minutes. She was red in the face, and looked completely miserable.

"What's up with you?" I asked her. "You've got a face like a wet week-end."

"We can't send the video to *You've Been Framed*," Fliss muttered.

"Why not?" we all said together.

"I just don't think it's a good idea," Fliss said stiffly.

"Oh, come on, Fliss, don't be a wimp all your life," Kenny urged. "If it does get on TV, we can get round our parents, no problem."

Fliss blushed. "It's not that."

"Well, what then?"

Fliss looked down at her feet. "I wasn't – er – actually filming Lyndz when she fell off the bed," she mumbled. "Sorry."

"What?" We all stared at her.

"You mean you missed the sleepover stunt of the century?" I said. "So what were you doing? Filming Kenny and Rosie on the other bed?"

"Um. No," said Fliss. "I *was* filming the teddy fights. Then I got bored..."

"So what were you filming then?" Rosie asked.

Fliss looked even more sheepish. "My cuddly toys on the windowsill."

"Oh, great big fat hairy deal," said Kenny in disgust. "So now we've got pathetic little cuddly toys in the middle of our radical sleepover vid."

"Plus we've lost the chance to win loads of money," I pointed out.

Lyndz shook her head sadly. "I really wanted to see myself somersaulting off the bed as well," she said.

"I said I was sorry," Fliss muttered miserably.

"Never mind, Fliss," Rosie said quickly.

"I've just thought of something." She turned to Lyndz. "You could do it again, couldn't you, Lyndz?"

"Do what again?" said Lyndz. I told you she was a bit slow on the uptake.

"Wobbling about on the edge of the bed, and somersaulting off it. You could do it again, couldn't you?"

Lyndz looked doubtful.

"I dunno—"

"Course you can!" Rosie grabbed Lyndz's arm, and hauled her onto Fliss's bed. "That's what we've got to do. Lyndz does the stunt again, and this time Fliss videos her!"

"Good idea!" Kenny slapped Rosie on the back. "Don't you think that's a good idea, Fliss?"

Fliss was suddenly looking a lot happier now that she was well and truly off the hook. "Yeah, good one. Come on then, Lyndz."

Lyndz picked up her teddy bear.

"OK, I'll give it a go." Then she frowned. "Isn't it cheating though?"

"No, course not," Kenny said. "I mean, it's not like you didn't do it at all, is it?"

"And anyway," I said, "I swear some of

those videos on the telly are set-ups."

"Well, all right," said Lyndz, and she climbed onto Fliss's bed. "Come on, then, Frankie."

I grabbed Stanley, and Rosie and Kenny sat down on the other bed to watch.

"I can't remember what we did first," said Lyndz. "I think I got in a few whacks at Stanley."

"And then I landed the killer thwack," I said. "That was the one that sent you off the bed. Ready, Fliss?"

"Ready," Fliss called back.

Lyndz and I began whacking each other's teddy bears again, like we'd done the first time. But it wasn't as easy as we thought it would be to do the stunt again. The trouble was, Lyndz was watching me like a hawk, waiting for the big THWACK! So I held off for a bit, then I swung Stanley at her teddy when she wasn't expecting it. Instead of falling spectacularly off the bed, though, Lyndz just sat down – plonk – on the duvet.

"Well, that was hilarious," Kenny said sarcastically.

"This is more difficult than it looks,

smarty-pants," I said.

"I told you I couldn't do it," Lyndz wailed.

"Try again," Fliss said.

Lyndz and I had a few more tries, but it was no good. Lyndz was just too nervous. I managed to knock her off the bed a few times, but there was nothing like the wobbling and somersaulting which had happened the first time. Lyndz was just too scared of hurting herself to try and do that again.

"This is hopeless," I said, after the sixth attempt. "Let's forget it."

"Sorry," Lyndz said, biting her lip.

"Let me and Rosie have a go." Kenny stood up. "I bet we can do it."

"But that's cheating," Lyndz said. "You didn't do it the first time."

"So what?" Kenny shrugged. "We want to get on the TV, don't we?"

"Yeah, but what about me and Lyndz?" I said.

"What about me and Rosie?" Kenny challenged me.

"Well, what about Fliss?" Lyndz chimed in. "She's stuck behind the camera."

We all looked at each other. It was becoming very obvious that, if we were going to send a Sleepover Club video to *You've Been Framed*, we all wanted to be in it.

"So that means we're all going to have to get into the video somehow," said Kenny.

"What, you mean we're all going to have a teddy fight and somersault off the bed at exactly the same time?" I asked sarcastically.

"Ha funny ha," said Kenny. "No, we'll do something else. Something screamingly funny, that we can all be in."

"Except the person who's doing the filming," said Fliss sulkily.

We all rolled our eyes at that.

"Hang on for just one tiny little second, Felicity Sidebotham," I said. "You said nobody was going to do any filming except you."

"I know," Fliss muttered. "But that was before I knew we were going to be on TV."

"Well, someone's got to work the camcorder," said Kenny. "If it's not Fliss, who's going to do it?"

We all looked down at our feet.

"Oh, go on," said Lyndz. "I'll do it. I don't mind."

65

Fliss looked relieved.

"Thanks, Lyndz. Come over here, and I'll show you how it works. It's dead easy."

"What are we going to do then?" Kenny said to me and Rosie, while Fliss and Lyndz were bent over the camcorder. "It's got to be funny to get on TV."

"They seem to like people falling over," said Rosie.

"And stunts with pets in," I said.

"Right," said Kenny. "Anyone fancy balancing Fliss's goldfish on their nose and then falling down the stairs?"

The three of us giggled.

"Whatever it is, it's got to be good," I said. "*You've Been Framed* must get loads of tapes."

"We could pretend we're sleepwalking," Rosie suggested. "Then we could do all sorts of daft things."

"What, four of us sleepwalking at the same time?" I said doubtfully. "I don't think that'll work."

Kenny's eyes lit up. "Wait a minute, I've got an excellent idea."

"What?" Rosie and I said together.

Kenny winked at us. "You'll have to wait and see. First I've got to try and persuade Fliss to let us go downstairs. There isn't enough room to do it here."

"No chance," Rosie said immediately.

"You obviously haven't seen Kenny sweet-talk anyone before," I muttered in Rosie's ear.

"Fliss, I've got a brilliant idea for our *You've Been Framed* video," Kenny said with a beaming smile.

Fliss raised her eyebrows. "Oh?"

Kenny nodded. "Yep, it's so brilliant, it's sure to get on TV."

Fliss began to look interested. "What is it?"

"Tell you in a minute," said Kenny. "The thing is, there's no room to do it in here. We need to go downstairs."

Fliss looked as though Kenny had asked her to cut her arm off.

"Are you crazy?" she spluttered. "We can't do that! What if my mum hears us?"

"She won't," Kenny said firmly. "Everyone's going to be really quiet."

"No!" Fliss hissed.

"We'll be as quiet as mice—"

"NO!"

"Oh, well, that's a shame." Kenny shrugged her shoulders. "Especially as you would've been the star."

Fliss's eyes widened.

"What?"

"Oh, didn't I say?" Kenny remarked innocently. "You were going to be the star of my idea. Still, never mind."

Fliss frowned. "Well, I suppose we could," she said slowly. "As long as everyone is really quiet…"

"Course we'll be quiet!" Kenny raced eagerly over to the bedroom door. "Come on then, let's go. Lyndz, are you sure you don't mind not being in the video?"

"Course I don't," Lyndz said cheerfully. She picked up the camcorder, and put it up to her eye. "Doing the filming is just as good."

"Come on then," said Kenny. "Let's go downstairs."

"And be quiet," Fliss added nervously.

We all tiptoed over to the door, our hearts thumping. Kenny turned the handle and pulled it open, and we all crept out one by one…

Look, we're not far from my house now, and I've still got the worst bit to tell you. We'd better stop along the way, 'cos I can't tell you what comes next if there's even a sniff of a parent around. Come on, let's sit down on this wall for a while.

CHAPTER SEVEN

Now, where was I? Oh, yeah, I'd just got to the bit where we were all creeping down the stairs, one behind the other. We didn't dare put the light on, so we were shuffling slowly along, trying not to trip over anything. I was in front, and Fliss was behind me, and then the others were behind her. I'm sort of like the Sleepover Club scout – I always get sent on ahead to sniff out the dangers. The others must think I'm dead brave. Or maybe I'm just the only one stupid enough to do it...

"Lyndz?" I heard Fliss whisper behind me. Then, "Ow! Kenny, you dweeb, you walked right into me!"

"Well, don't just stop like that!" I heard Kenny grumbling. "I can't see a thing in the dark."

"I just wanted to ask Lyndz if the camcorder's OK," Fliss whispered.

"What?" That was Lyndz. She was at the end of the line with the camera. "I can't hear you!"

I rolled my eyes. This was getting ridiculous. "Kenny, Fliss wants to ask Lyndz if the camcorder's OK. Pass it on."

Kenny turned round, and whispered.

"Rosie, Fliss wants to know if the camcorder's OK. Pass it on."

We all stood and waited for Rosie to whisper to Lyndz. A few seconds later an answer came back from Kenny.

"The camcorder's fine. It's just got a bit of a headache, that's all."

"Oh, very funny," Fliss said under her breath. The rest of us began to giggle as silently as we could.

"Well, honestly, Fliss," said Kenny. "Keep cool, can't you? It's only a machine, not a person."

"Can we please get a move on?" I hissed.

"If Fliss's mum hears us, we're history."

We carried on shuffling down the stairs, and then we groped our way across the hall and into the living room. I counted in four shadowy figures, and then I closed the door as silently as I could. We waited, holding our breath and listening hard, but no one came. So I flipped the light switch on.

"Let me see the camcorder, Lyndz." Straightaway Fliss rushed over and grabbed the camcorder.

"It's fine," said Lyndz. "Did you think I'd taken a bite out of it on the way downstairs, or something?"

"I just want to be sure," said Fliss. You can see why we call her Fusspot.

"Your mum's got loads of stuff, Fliss," said Rosie. She was standing behind the sofa, looking at a china lady in a green dress, which stood on a small table.

"Don't touch anything," Fliss said nervously. "My mum'll get in a real razz if anything gets broken. Some of these things cost a lot of money."

We all looked round the living room. I think I've told you about it before, haven't I?

It's like every other room in Fliss's house, all neat and clean and cream-coloured. And there are hundreds and hundreds of ornaments everywhere, things like china ladies wearing old-fashioned costumes, toby jugs and big glass bowls. There are so many things in it, you're almost frightened to move, in case you accidentally knock something over. Fliss is always going on about how much her mum's stuff cost, but some of it looked pretty nasty to me, although I was too polite to say so. That china lady in the green dress that Rosie was looking at, for instance, was gross.

"Let's get started," said Lyndz with an enormous yawn. "I'm going to fall asleep soon if we don't."

"Come on then, Kenny." I looked at her. "What's this super-cool plan of yours to get us on *You've Been Framed* then?"

Kenny grinned.

"A Human Pyramid," she said.

We all looked at each other.

"Excuse me?" I said. "I thought you said a Human Pyramid."

"I did."

73

"What, you mean when people stand on each other's shoulders?" Rosie asked.

"I've seen that on the telly," said Lyndz. "Only the people at the bottom were riding about on motorbikes, with the others standing on top of them."

Fliss was looking a bit sick. "Do you think that's going to work, Kenny?"

"Just a minute, give me a chance to explain," Kenny said confidently. "We won't be able to do it exactly right—"

"You're telling me," I remarked. "It's going to be a pretty sad human pyramid with only four of us."

"I know that," Kenny said. "I suppose I was thinking more of a Human Tower."

"A Human Tower?" Rosie repeated.

"Yep, one person's at the bottom, and then someone climbs up and sits on their shoulders, and then someone sits on *their* shoulders and so on." Kenny beamed at us. "What do you think?"

"It'll never work," said Lyndz.

"That's the point," Kenny said triumphantly. "We want it to go wrong, don't we? Then it'll be funny. Trust me."

When Kenny says "Trust me", it's like telling someone to trust Count Dracula when he's feeling a bit peckish. We all looked nervously at each other.

"Who's the unlucky idiot who's going to be at the bottom holding everyone else up?" I asked. Kenny grinned at me. "Oh no, you're joking."

"Well, you are the tallest, Frankie." Kenny said cheerfully. "And the strongest."

"Who'll be at the very top then?" asked Lyndz.

Kenny shrugged.

"It's got to be Fliss, who else?" She beamed at Fliss. "See, I told you you'd be the star."

Fliss looked a bit more cheerful. "Well, I suppose we could give it a go," she said.

Kenny looked thoughtfully up at the chandelier light fitting in the middle of the room.

"If we can get up high enough, Fliss could swing across the room like Tarzan on her mum's chandelier."

Now Fliss didn't look quite so keen.

"Kenny—" she began.

"Oh, come on, Kenny," I said. "Be serious."

75

Kenny grinned. "OK, I was only joking."

Fliss heaved a huge sigh of relief. "Are you ready with the camera, Lyndz?" she said.

Lyndz put the camera to her eye, and gave us a thumbs-up.

"Right, me first then," Kenny jumped up onto the arm of the sofa, and grabbed my shoulders. "Bend down a bit, Frankie, and let me climb onto you."

"Why do I always have to be the one who does all the hard bits?" I grumbled, but I crouched down and let Kenny get onto my shoulders, with her legs dangling in front. It was a bit difficult to stand up with Kenny's dead weight on top of me but I just about managed it.

"See?" Kenny waved at the others, and began bouncing up and down on my shoulders with excitement. "I told you it'd work – woh! Stand still, Frankie!"

I was trying to stand still, but my knees kept buckling under me, and I couldn't stop myself staggering from side to side.

"Ow!" I complained as Kenny grabbed at my hair. "I'm going to be bald soon at this rate!"

"Well, keep still, can't you?" Kenny hissed. "If you didn't keep moving around, I wouldn't have to hold on. Now bend down so Rosie can get onto my back."

I tried to bend down, but I couldn't. My knees kept on wobbling and I was scared I was going to fall over. I could hardly hold Kenny up, and Rosie and Fliss had to get on board yet.

Fliss had now gone right off the idea. She was dancing round us, looking more and more agitated. "Stop it!" she was wailing. "You're going to break something!"

Kenny ignored her.

"Come on, Rosie! Climb up onto my shoulders!"

My knees went before Rosie even made a move. I collapsed onto the sofa, throwing Kenny head first into a pile of cushions.

"Ouch!" Kenny complained, pulling herself upright. "What's the matter with you lot? That would have been excellent."

"Yeah, if I was Arnie Schwarzenegger," I said, rubbing my aching shoulders.

"You're crazy, Kenny," said Rosie. "It's too risky. We might break something."

"Yes," said Fliss, glaring at Kenny. "Now sit down where I can keep an eye on you."

We all sat down meekly on the cream-coloured sofa. Lyndz yawned, which started us all off.

"I'm so tired," Lyndz complained. "Let's forget it and go to bed."

"We can't forget about being on TV!" said Fliss. "This might be the only chance we ever get." She looked round at us, a little smile on her lips. "Actually, I've got an idea…"

"For *You've Been Framed*?" I said. That made us all sit up and stop yawning. "What is it?"

"It's really funny," said Fliss.

We all leant forward eagerly on the sofa.

"Tell us then," said Rosie.

"Well, first I'll have to go into the kitchen," said Fliss.

"Are we going to do some cooking like we did at the last sleepover here then?" asked Lyndz.

"You mean when Fliss's porridge went mad in the microwave?" I said.

"Oh, and remember Lyndz set off the smoke alarm when she was making toast," said Kenny.

"I nearly died laughing when Kenny's waffle mixture went walkies out of the waffle-maker," said Rosie. That started us all laughing, even Fliss.

"Now that would have been a brilliant video to send to *You've Been Framed*!" I said. "We'd have got on TV, no problem!"

"So are we going to do some more cooking then?" Lyndz asked eagerly.

"No." Fliss shook her head. "I'm just going into the kitchen to get some orange squash and biscuits."

"Great," said Kenny. "I'm starving."

"What about your *You've Been Framed* idea?" Lyndz asked.

"This *is* my idea," Fliss said impatiently. "I'll get the squash and biscuits, and hand them round. Then when I get to Kenny, I'll drop the plate and tip the biscuits all over her."

"And?" I said.

Fliss frowned. "There's no 'and'," she said. "That's it."

"That's IT?" I repeated. "That's IT?"

"It's not very funny, Fliss," Lyndz said. She was trying to be polite. What she really

79

meant was that it wasn't funny at all.

"Of course it is," Fliss said confidently. "What do you think, Rosie?"

Rosie cleared her throat a couple of times.

"Well – um – it might be funny, I suppose…" Her voice died away.

"I think it's a great idea," Kenny said unexpectedly. "I reckon we should give it a go."

My mouth fell open. I couldn't believe what I'd just heard. Fliss's idea was rubbish, so why wasn't Kenny saying so? What was she up to?

"Are you sure, Kenny?" Lyndz asked hesitantly.

Kenny nodded. "Yeah, I think it'll be excellent."

Fliss beamed at her. "Thanks, Kenny!" she said gratefully. "I'll go and get the squash and biscuits. Lyndz, get ready with the camera."

"We'll be ready," Kenny promised. "Oh, and Fliss, put some ice cubes in the orange squash, will you? I'm really hot and thirsty."

Fliss went off to the kitchen, smiling all over her face. Rosie went to help her, and Lyndz started fiddling with the camcorder, so that left me and Kenny on our own.

"What was all that about?" I asked.

"What do you mean?" Kenny said innocently.

"All that stuff with Fliss." I looked at Kenny closely. "You're up to something, Laura MacKenzie."

"Oh dear, what a suspicious mind you've got, Francesca Thomas." Kenny leaned back on the sofa, and put her hands behind her head. "As if I'd be up to anything."

I wasn't convinced. After all, I knew Kenny. But I couldn't see what on earth she was going to do. After all, there wasn't a lot that could go wrong with some orange squash and a plate of biscuits, was there? I mean, not even Kenny could manage to create a disaster out of that.

Could she?

CHAPTER EIGHT

Fliss and Rosie were in the kitchen for what seemed like ages, but eventually Rosie came out.

"Fliss says she's ready to bring the tray of squash and biscuits in," she announced. "She wants me, Frankie and Kenny sitting on the sofa, and Lyndz ready with the camera."

Lyndz gave Rosie a thumbs-up.

"I'm ready."

"So are we," Kenny said. "Did Fliss remember to put some ice cubes in the squash?"

Rosie nodded, and sat down next to me.

"What's with the ice cubes?" I said in

Kenny's ear. "That's the second time you've mentioned them."

Kenny shrugged.

"I'm just thirsty, that's all."

"We're not supposed to be stuffing our faces here, you know," I reminded her.

Kenny stuck her tongue out at me. "So what? I can still get a drink, can't I?"

I looked hard at her. There was something going on, but for the life of me I couldn't see what it was. I didn't have time to say anything else, because right at that moment Fliss popped her head round the kitchen door.

"I'm ready," she said, nodding at Lyndz. "Let's try and get it right first time, or we'll be running out of tape."

We all nodded solemnly. Personally, I couldn't see that it mattered whether we ran out of tape or not. Fliss spilling a plate of biscuits over Kenny was hardly going to provide laugh-a-minute stuff for a TV programme. But it was easier to sit there and do it than to argue with Fliss, so I stayed where I was between Rosie and Kenny.

Fliss came out of the kitchen with a silly

smile on her face. She was carrying a large blue tray which held four glasses, a plate of Hobnobs and a big jug of orange squash with ice cubes in it. It took her a while to get across to the sofa where we were sitting because she kept stopping to smile at the camera. But she made it eventually.

"Would everyone like some squash and biscuits?" she asked brightly, putting the tray down on the coffee table.

"Yes, please," we all chorused dutifully.

"I'll hand the biscuits round first," Fliss said meaningfully. She had her back to Lyndz, and she started winking at Kenny like mad. Kenny grinned at her, and nodded.

"Would you like a biscuit, Rosie?" Fliss asked, picking up the plate. I suppose she was going to ask me next, and then would come the Big Moment when she tipped the biscuits all over Kenny. Hilarious. But, of course, we didn't get that far. Rosie didn't even get a chance to reply to Fliss's question.

Because, as soon as Fliss turned to offer Rosie one of the Hobnobs, Kenny pounced. She leaned forward, scooped a couple of ice cubes out of the jug of squash and tipped them down the neck of Fliss's pyjama jacket.

From that moment on, everything moved so fast I'm still not sure what really happened. Of course, Fliss leapt a mile into the air when the ice cubes connected with her bare skin, although by some miracle she managed not to scream. When she leapt a mile, though, she still had the plate in her hand. Biscuits flew everywhere, as Fliss accidentally cracked the plate hard against Rosie's chin. Rosie gasped, and flung out her arms in shock. I was sitting next to her, and I didn't want to get hit in the eye, did I? So I leapt backwards onto the top of the sofa, out of harm's way.

Silly me. I leapt too hard. I teetered and wobbled on the top of the sofa for a few seconds, a bit like Lyndz had done on the bed earlier, and then I went over. My heels flew over my head, and I landed on the thick, fluffy carpet on the other side. Unfortunately I hit the little table on my way over, and I took the painted china lady in the nasty green dress with me. Well, most of her. Her head fell off when she hit the floor, and it rolled away under the dresser.

Feeling a bit dazed, I pulled myself upright. Four horrified faces were hanging over the sofa, looking down at me and at the headless body of the painted china lady lying next to me. In fact, Fliss's face was exactly the same nasty green colour as the lady's dress.

"Frankie, what have you done?" Rosie gasped.

"Me!" I said indignantly. "It wasn't my fault. Thanks a lot, Kenny."

"Sorry, Fliss," Kenny muttered. "I didn't know that was going to happen, did I?"

Fliss was almost crying.

"My mum's going to kill me. That ornament cost eighty pounds!"

"Calm down, Fliss," I said. "We might be able to fix it."

"Where's the head gone?" Lyndz asked.

"I think it rolled under the dresser," I said.

Kenny climbed off the sofa.

"I'll have a look." She lay down on the carpet, and pushed her arm under the dresser as far as it would go. "Got it!"

She pulled the lady's head out, and we all crowded round to look at it. Apart from the fact that it wasn't attached to her body anymore, there wasn't any other damage.

"Look, it'll be easy to repair it," Lyndz said, taking the head from Kenny and the body from me. "It broke off right around the neckline of the dress."

We all looked. Lyndz was right. It had been a clean break.

"We can fix it, Fliss," Lyndz said kindly, "And your mum will never even notice it's been broken, I swear."

"Really?" Fliss sniffed.

"No problem," said Lyndz. "But we need some glue."

Fliss frowned. "I'm not allowed to use the superglue," she said. "But I've got a Pritt stick in my school bag. Will that do?"

Lyndz nodded, and Fliss went out to fetch it.

"You seem to know a lot about mending things, Lyndz," Rosie said admiringly.

Lyndz shrugged. "When you've got four brothers, you get used to it," she said.

Fliss came back with the Pritt stick, and Lyndz carefully rubbed it over the top of the body and the bottom of the head. The rest of us picked up the broken biscuits, and then swept up the crumbs. Then we had to sit and wait for the pieces to stick. It took ages, even though we all took turns at pressing the two halves together. By this time it was 1.30 am, and we were all dead tired.

At last Lyndz said she thought the bits had stuck. We did a few tests like turning the lady upside down ten times in a row to see if the head fell off or not. It didn't.

Lyndz put the lady gently down on the coffee-table, and we all stood back and looked at it. It was amazing. You just couldn't tell that it had ever been broken. Well, only if you got down on your hands and knees and took a close look.

"Thanks, Lyndz," Fliss said gratefully. "You've saved my life."

"So can we please go to bed now?" Kenny said with an enormous yawn.

"We could have gone to bed ages ago if you hadn't been such an idiot," Fliss retorted with a sniff.

"OK, OK," said Kenny. "I said sorry, didn't I?"

"Sorry isn't enough," said Fliss. "You can be my slave for a week."

Kenny groaned. "Oh, all right then."

Fliss's eyes gleamed. I could tell that she was already starting to think up tasks for Kenny to perform.

"I *have* to go to bed NOW," said Rosie. "I'm falling asleep on my feet."

"I'm going to have some squash first." Kenny picked up the jug, and poured herself a glassful. "Oh, rats, all the ice cubes have melted."

"I should think you've had enough of ice cubes for a while," I remarked.

"I have," said Rosie. "And I never want to see *You've Been Framed* again, either."

"I never want to see a camcorder again," I said between yawns. "Ever."

"Where is the camcorder?" Fliss asked suddenly, looking wild-eyed with panic.

"It's OK, I turned it off when Frankie went over the sofa," Lyndz said. "I left it over there on the chair."

Lyndz went over to get it, but just as she bent over to pick the camcorder up, we all got a shock.

The living-room door was flung wide open.

CHAPTER NINE

Fliss's mum was standing in the doorway, blinking at us. We all nearly dropped down dead with shock.

"What on earth are you girls doing down here?" Mrs Sidebotham exclaimed. "It's a quarter to two!"

"Sorry, Mrs Sidebotham," we all mumbled. Out of the corner of my eye, I saw Lyndz sit down carefully in the armchair, so that the camcorder was hidden behind her. Meanwhile, Kenny had moved slightly closer to me, so that we were shoulder to shoulder and blocking Mrs Sidebotham's view of the china lady in the green dress who now had a broken neck.

"Well?" Mrs Sidebotham raised her eyebrows at us.

"We woke up and felt hungry," Fliss said quickly.

"And thirsty," Kenny chimed in.

"So we came downstairs for some squash and biscuits," Rosie finished off.

Mrs Sidebotham looked suspicious.

"You haven't been doing any cooking, have you?" she asked.

We all shook our heads virtuously.

"No, Mrs Sidebotham."

"Good." Fliss's mum looked mightily relieved. "Off to bed then, please. I don't know what your parents would think if they knew you were up at this time of night."

Yawning, we all stumbled over to the door. Except for Lyndz. She stayed where she was in the armchair.

"Come on, Lyndsey," said Fliss's mum impatiently. "Time for bed."

Lyndz stood up reluctantly. I guessed she was waiting for Mrs Sidebotham to go out of the room first, so she could grab the camcorder and bring it upstairs with her. But it was obvious that Fliss's mum wasn't going anywhere until she'd checked us all one by one.

As Lyndz came over to the door, we all looked anxiously at the chair where she'd been sitting. Fliss was standing next to me and I could feel her shaking in complete panic. But we needn't have worried. There was no sign of the camcorder anywhere. There was a big, fat, green cushion in the middle of the armchair, and somehow Lyndz must have managed to shove the camcorder behind it.

We all gave such a sigh of relief at exactly the same moment that I'm surprised Mrs Sidebotham didn't notice it. But then she wouldn't have. She was too busy staring at her painted china lady in the green dress.

"What have you girls been up to down here?" she asked suspiciously. "You've moved my Victorian lady."

We all froze to the spot. Fliss's knees were shaking so much, I swear it was only Rosie and me standing shoulder to shoulder on either side of her that held her up. The only one of us who had the nerve to say anything at all was Kenny.

"Oh, sorry, Mrs Sidebotham. That was my fault."

We all turned to stare at Kenny in amazement, and if looks could kill, Fliss would have murdered Kenny on the spot. But Kenny didn't take any notice.

"It's so pretty, I picked it up to have a closer look at it," she went on. "I hope you don't mind."

Fliss's mum looked pleased.

"Yes, it is pretty, isn't it? I don't mind you looking at my things, Laura, but do be careful, won't you?" She reached out, and turned the figure slightly to the left. Holding it by its head. We all watched in breathless terror. We expected the head to come off in her hands like something in a horror movie, but it didn't.

"Now – BED," said Fliss's mum firmly, and we all scrambled up the stairs as fast as we could. None of us could believe quite how lucky we'd been that evening, and the sooner we were all tucked up in bed, the better. Besides, we were all asleep on our feet.

Fliss's mum came with us, and watched us

crawl into our beds and sleeping bags. "Now I don't want to hear a sound until morning," she warned us. "Not a single sound."

I yawned hugely. I wasn't going to argue with that. I'd never felt so tired in my whole life. Mrs Sidebotham switched the light out, and went away.

Then Fliss said in a low voice, "Lyndz, what did you do with the camcorder?"

"I shoved it behind the cushion," Lyndz said sleepily. "I couldn't think what else to do."

"We can't leave it there," Kenny said. "It's still got our tape in it."

"I'll go down and get it in a few minutes," Fliss said, in between yawns. "When my mum's gone to sleep again."

There was silence for a little while. No one even suggested singing our sleepover song because we were just too worn out. I curled up snugly inside my sleeping bag, and closed my eyes. What a night.

I started to drift off into sleep. But then Kenny, who was lying on the floor next to me, began to giggle softly.

"Shut up, MacKenzie," I said drowsily.

"Sorry," Kenny muttered. "I was just remembering Fliss's face when I dropped those ice cubes down her neck."

I thought back to that moment, and a picture of Fliss's horrified face swam into my mind too. I began to laugh, and I had to turn over and bury my face in my pillow.

"What are you two sniggering at?" asked Lyndz, who was lying on the other side of me.

"Fliss's face when those ice cubes went down her neck!" I blurted out between giggles. Kenny was too paralysed with laughter to say anything herself. There was silence for a few seconds, and then Lyndz's sleeping bag began to shake too.

"Shut up, you lot!" Rosie whispered. "I'm trying to get to sleep here!"

"What about when Fliss cracked Rosie on the chin with the plate of biscuits?" Lyndz spluttered helplessly. That set the three of us off again, and this time Rosie couldn't help joining in. We were practically all weeping with laughter.

"Shut up," said Fliss from the other bed. "I don't think it was very funny at all. Any of it."

"What, not even when Frankie went over the back of the sofa?" Kenny said. "With her arms and legs, she looked like a daddy-long-legs having a fit."

This time we all laughed, even Fliss. We just couldn't help ourselves. We laughed for ages. And we still had smiles on our faces when we fell asleep.

So now you know just about everything. You also know why we don't want anyone to find out what really happened last night. You can keep a secret, can't you? Course you can! You'd better – or I'll set Kenny on you.

Only kidding. I know I can trust you.

Well, there isn't really that much left for me to tell you. We all overslept this morning, because of going to bed so late last night. Usually we like getting up early when we sleepover at Fliss's because her mum makes great breakfasts. They've got a juicer and the famous waffle-maker, so we always pig out. But not this morning.

Even Andy and Fliss's mum overslept. The only one who didn't was Fliss's little brother Callum, who didn't bother waking anyone else up. Typical. We were all still snoring away when Kenny's dad arrived at ten o'clock to collect her, so the first we knew about it was Callum banging on Fliss's bedroom door. I was getting a lift home with Kenny, so I had to get up too.

"You look like the walking dead," Kenny remarked as we shoved our stuff into our sleepover bags.

"Yeah, well, you'd win a Miss Baggy-Eyes contest, no problem," I said.

The others were still dead to the world. Rosie opened one eye and said goodbye to us, but Fliss and Lyndz were just lumps under the bedclothes. Yawning, Kenny and I staggered out onto the landing, just as Fliss's mum hurried out of her bedroom.

"I'm sorry, girls," she gasped. "We should have been up hours ago. I'll make you some breakfast."

"It's OK, Mrs Sidebotham," Kenny said politely. "My dad's here to collect us."

"Oh dear." Fliss's mum looked guilty. "What on earth is he going to think?"

Kenny shrugged. "Don't worry about it," she said. But when we got downstairs, where

97

Kenny's dad was waiting in the hall, Mrs Sidebotham spent about ten minutes apologising for oversleeping.

"—and the girls never even got to watch their sleepover video!" she finished up. "I was looking forward to seeing that myself."

Kenny and I glanced at each other. Whoops. I didn't think Mrs Sidebotham would be that keen on the video if she saw the uncensored version. Anyway, she wouldn't be seeing it at all because Fliss would have collected the camcorder from behind the cushion and replaced our tape with a blank one by now.

"Oh, well, never mind." Dr MacKenzie opened the front door. "They can watch it another time. Are you ready, girls?"

"Thanks for having us, Mrs Sidebotham," we said politely, then we legged it down the path, and jumped into the car. For once, I was going to be glad to get home.

"I feel like I could sleep for a week," Kenny muttered in my ear.

"Me too," I said. "I was so tired last night, I didn't even hear Fliss go downstairs to get the camcorder."

"Me neither," Kenny said.

We looked at each other.

"But she must have done," Kenny went on confidently. "She wouldn't have forgotten."

"No," I agreed.

When I got home, my mum took one look at me and started tutting.

"Late night, Frankie?"

"What makes you think that?" I said.

"You could carry home ten pounds of potatoes in those bags under your eyes." My mum looked at me critically. "How was your video?"

"All right." I managed to look her straight in the eye. "We didn't get a chance to watch it though, because we all overslept."

"What a shame," my mum said. "Oh, well, you'll be pleased to know that your dad's now thinking of buying a camcorder. I've tried to put him off, but you know what your dad's like. He gets an idea into his head, and then it sticks." She smiled at me. "A bit like someone else I know."

"Oh, Mum," I yawned. "Dad's crazy. Camcorders are so over-rated. They're not that cool, really."

My mum looked at me suspiciously.

"You've changed your tune. What happened at Fliss's last night?"

"Oh, nothing," I said cautiously. "But once you've seen one camcorder, you've seen them all."

So that was that. I think my mum was a bit suspicious about what had gone on at Fliss's sleepover, but when nothing happened (Fliss's mum didn't ring up to complain, like she usually did), she stopped worrying. Anyway, my mum and I ganged up on my dad and told him that instead of having a camcorder, we'd rather use all that money to go on holiday.

So everything turned out all right in the end, didn't it? There aren't many sleepovers when that happens. I'm well in with Mum because nothing disastrous happened at the sleepover (or so she thinks), and also because we've persuaded my dad not to buy a camcorder. And I'm going on holiday. Excellent!

Look, that's my house at the end of the street. Why don't you come home and watch *Mrs Doubtfire* with us? My dad's making the famous Thomas pizza, and we've got popcorn and lemonade too. And I know you won't say a word to my parents about what I just told you.

Wait a minute, though.

See that red car parked outside our house?

Do you know whose car that is?

I do.

It's Fliss's mum's car.

GOODBYE

Panic stations! What do you think Fliss's mum is doing at my house? Yes, she knows my mum, and yes, she does call round sometimes, but it's a bit of a coincidence that she's calling round the night after a sleepover. Especially a sleepover when something completely drastic happened...

Maybe I left something at Fliss's house after the sleepover, and her mum's come to return it? No, I know I didn't. I remember unpacking everything.

So what's Fliss's mum doing at my house? It must be something important if she's come round to see my parents in person, rather than just phoning up. Something important or something serious...

What did you say? No, that can't be right. Fliss couldn't be so stupid... I mean, she said she was going to wait a few minutes until her mum was asleep again, and then she was going to go downstairs and get the camcorder back. I'm sure she wouldn't have forgotten. And if she'd got the camcorder, she definitely wouldn't have forgotten to take our tape out and put a new blank tape in. Fliss is too scared of getting into trouble with her mum to have forgotten to make sure we were in the clear.

But then again, we were all really tired, including Fliss... Maybe she was planning to go downstairs, and she just fell asleep without meaning to? Kenny and I should have checked this morning when we were getting ready to leave, but we were in a hurry to go home and Fliss didn't even wake up. Oh no. Do you think that the camcorder was still hidden behind the cushion this morning?

No, I don't believe it. Fliss must have gone downstairs after the rest of us were asleep. We just didn't hear her, that's all. Come on, we don't have to be nervous. Let's just go home calmly and sensibly, and find out exactly what Fliss's mum is doing here.

Quick, get behind that tree! Mrs Sidebotham's coming out of our house right now!

Did she see us? No, she's going over to her car. Can you see her face? What does she look like? Normal? Happy? Sad? Or just plain, downright FURIOUS? There's only one way to find out. I'll have to go home.

But you'll come with me, won't you? It's probably better if you don't come in at first, just in case mum and dad are waiting to tear me to bits. But I'm sure they won't be. I hope.

Here we are then. Why don't you go and wait by the living-room window, then you can see what's going on? If everything's OK, I'll give you a thumbs-up. Wish me luck!

The door opens. It's my mum.

"Oh, it's you, Frankie. You were a long time."

I look at my mum closely. She seems OK. She's not red in the face, and she's not glaring at me. That's a good sign.

"Sorry," I say. "It took me a really long time

to choose a video."

"What did you get?" my mum asks.

"*Mrs Doubtfire.*" I hold the video out to show her. "I know we've seen it before, but you liked it so much, I thought I'd get it out again." Crawl, crawl.

"Good idea." My mum opens the door wider, and I go inside. But hang on a minute, we're not in the clear yet.

As soon as I see my dad pacing up and down the living room, I know that something's not quite right. My dad's not as good as my mum at keeping a straight face. I think you'd better stay outside the window for the moment. I've got a feeling things could start getting nasty in here.

"What video did you get, Frankie?" my dad asks in a voice that tells me something not very nice is about to happen.

"*Mrs Doubtfire*," I say cautiously. No use going looking for trouble, as my grandma always says, let it come and look for you. And, boy, was it coming to look for me right now.

"Oh, *Mrs Doubtfire*'s a brilliant film," my mum says. "But we've got an even better video than *Mrs Doubtfire* to show you."

"Oh?" I say, with a sinking heart. Now I know exactly why Fliss's mum had come round to our house.

"Sit down." says my dad.

"Well, actually, I don't feel much like watching a video right now," I start babbling nervously. "I think I'll go up to my room—"

"Sit down, Frankie," my mum says grimly.

I sit.

My dad picks up the remote control, and turns the TV on. A very familiar scene fills the TV screen. That's Kenny, Rosie and me, sitting in a row on Mrs Sidebotham's cream-coloured sofa. Then the camera swings round a little jerkily to show Fliss coming out of the kitchen, beaming all over her face and carrying a tray of orange squash and biscuits. We all watch in silence as Fliss puts the tray down on the coffee table, and then picks up the plate of biscuits. She turns to offer the biscuits to Rosie, and there, just at the very side of the picture, we can see Kenny's fingers dip into the jug of orange squash, and pull out some ice cubes. Then we see Kenny jump up and tip the ice down

Fliss's pyjama jacket.

I have to say that Lyndz would make a great film director when she grows up. She had managed to catch Fliss's horrified face perfectly, right in the middle of the screen, followed by the plate cracking against Rosie's chin. Then the camera had followed me quickly as I jumped up onto the back of the sofa, and it had captured my fall to the carpet in every detail. There is just one more shot of me in a heap on the floor with the headless figure of the china lady next to me, and then the picture goes black. That must have been when Lyndz switched the camera off.

No one says anything. Even though I know I'm now in deep doom forever, I just want to laugh my head off. I've never seen anything as funny as that video, not even on *You've Been Framed*. It's a classic. But I dare not even smile. If I do, I know I'll be in even bigger trouble.

When it's finally over, my dad turns off the TV.

"I think you'd better go to your room," says my mum. "We'll talk about this later when you've had time to think over what you've done."

Oh no, I hate it when they do that. Why can't they just give me my punishment now? At least then I know what I'm letting myself in for. But I'd better not argue.

I go quietly out of the room. Look, I think you'd better go. I'm going to be grounded for at least a year, so there's no point in you hanging around any more. Still, it was almost worth being grounded just to see that video. It's a shame we'll never get to send it to *You've Been Framed* now. I bet we would have got on TV, no problem.

As I'm going upstairs, I hear funny noises coming from the living-room. So I tiptoe back down, to find out what's going on. I put my ear to the door, and listen.

Guess what?

My mum and dad are laughing their heads off!

"Frankie and the others are going to have to pay for that figure they broke," my mum is saying.

My dad is too busy laughing to reply for a few seconds.

"Come on, let's watch it again. I've never seen anything as hilarious in my whole life!"

I hear the sound of the video being rewound, and then the sound of my mum and dad laughing again.

"That's just a classic," says my dad. "You know what? It's a shame we can't send this to *You've Been Framed*. I'm sure they'd show it."

I couldn't believe what I was hearing. Parents! Aren't they enough to make you sick?

But maybe that means I'll get off without being grounded for the rest of my life.

Wish me luck.

See ya!

Order Form

To order direct from the publishers, just make a list of the titles you want and fill in the form below:

Name ....

Address ....

....

....

Send to: Dept 6, HarperCollins Publishers Ltd, Westerhill Road, Bishopbriggs, Glasgow G64 2QT.

Please enclose a cheque or postal order to the value of the cover price, plus:

UK & BFPO: Add £1.00 for the first book, and 25p per copy for each additional book ordered.

Overseas and Eire: Add £2.95 service charge. Books will be sent by surface mail but quotes for airmail despatch will be given on request.

A 24-hour telephone ordering service is available to holders of Visa, MasterCard, Amex or Switch cards on 0141- 772 2281.

HarperCollins *Children's Books*